FLY OVER
THIS
stories from the new Midwest

**FLY OVER
THIS**
stories from the new Midwest

by Ryan Elliott Smith

Tortoise Books
Chicago, IL

Published in the United States by Tortoise Books.
www.tortoisebooks.com

ISBN 978-1948954631

Cover design by Ryan Elliott Smith
Tortoise Books Logo ©2022 by Tortoise Books.
Original artwork by Rachele O'Hare.

This, like everything else,
is only done with Allison's support.
Neither it, nor I, would be what we are without her.

And to Ottawa, IL.
No matter what I say in here, I love you,
am proud of what you've become,
and to you, also owe so much of who I am.

AUTHOR'S NOTE

In these stories, you will find grammar choices and sentence constructions that are uncommon in fiction. That is why they are there. If you are among those who are on the stricter side when it comes to such matters, those choices, along with several other seldomly published turns of phrase, may feel strange in your mouth. But they do not in mine.

Some of the folks I grew up with do sound like me. Many do not. But everywhere I've been and everyone I've known over the course of my life has shaped the way I talk. That way is celebrated here.

So, in these stories, it is my sincere hope that folks who grew up where I did, or in small towns just like it all over America, hear themselves in these stories. I wrote this book this way for them. More than anything else, even if only for a moment, I hope they hear their voices, and the voices of their families, lovingly depicted here.

Further, I called the book *Fly Over This* because I believe that if we can identify the reasons we treat the middle of this country with such open, but relatively harmless prejudice, we may be better equipped to identify those other darker, much more horrible prejudices that lurk in some of us, even in some of those people we love, even in ourselves. Such a title and this approach to writing is *supposed* to be antagonistic to *any* one way of thinking. I hope it is.

stories from the new Midwest

"Somewhere back there in the dust,
that same small town in each of us."

– Don Henley, "The End of the Innocence"

THAT DAY WHERE
YOU LIVE

I picked Shawn up in the early afternoon at his mom's house, a little high. He was super cut and skinny then, still a wrestler, and one of the few varsity teammates of mine that could grow a really good, full beard. His was a red one, one that made him look like those gritty, Depression-era ballplayers that rarely saw an inning but certainly appeared as though they were just born for the game. His face still carries in its wide and bulbous bones that recent immigrant look. It is still punctured with the dimples that got him attention from the occasional girl when we were young, but through the pictures I've seen of him on his Facebook friend requests, I've noticed over the years that he's gotten old fast. He's had a ton of kids, has let himself go, and has clearly given up on something important. Although I can't say with any accuracy what exactly it is, it almost certainly says nothing good about me.

There it is again, this Facebook friend request of his that I never accept. In the twenty years since I'd wrestled with him, the first thing I noticed was that he'd gone bald young and gotten pretty overweight. But recently, I thought he was taking better care of himself. There was a picture of him running, one on a Divvy somewhere along Chicago's lakeshore path, one in front of this Vitamix sloshing with green slurry. Now he's all thinned out, looks like he's prepping for a divorce, but the images of him are more haunting my page than anything else. Loitering, this ignored request keeps showing up and there Shawn is, smiling at me in his techy, casual clothes, these same Wayfarer knockoffs on, looking – I have to admit – kind of fantastic, always in a bright sun. The thing is, I can't be the only one judging him every time his picture is switched out for one taken of his litter of dirty babies wrangling him like a steer. I know the picture I chose to use on FB was a better choice. It was taken after I'd had pneumonia for a little over a week and had recently broken up with someone. I was looking pretty good for me, a little gaunt maybe, but with sunglasses hiding my still sick eyes, it was better than I'd looked in a while. When I uploaded the shot, I thought about it a ton. I was certain that the picture would increase my chances of getting laid someday somehow.

It didn't.

But now there's a message from this girl he married, Erica Strout. I stare at that notification for a second, too, but do eventually open it to read that she wishes she would have seen me at Shawn's wake. She says that she has a CD I'd given him, this Beatles CD I gave him the day the two of them first hung out, the day I picked Shawn up at his mom's. Punching way above my weight, it was me that was interested in Erica then, but it was Shawn that blasted right out his front door he was so revved up. His cigarettes fell out the front pocket of his shirt. He bent over, snatched them up, and it was obvious that he wasn't wearing any underwear. Neither was I. This was our habit for when we knew we would be around girls. Shawn and I had a standing rule to always do without in order to appear too cool for underwear, and, thus, what we lamely hoped was more irresistible to all the ladies. We had no idea that this was going to be a problem until after we went to meet up with Erica and dove off a 70 ft. cliff just outside Oglesby, Illinois.

Shawn stood in his yard trying to light this Zippo by snapping his fingers, a technique he'd spent several months of our junior year working to perfect. He'd nearly gotten it to where he could do it on his first try, but ended up snapping for a fourth or fifth time when a lazy blue flag of fire rolled out. He waved it under his smoke, managed to light only half of it up as he got in my car.

We took off.

We wanted to get an early start. I'd skipped most the day, left school at maybe noon, had spent the early afternoon waxing and using the good shammy on my Camaro. I sat in the driveway with the t-tops off, my parents at work and trusting I was at school, weed sizzling on my lips. I had glossed my dash right with Maguire's for impending company and Shawn was running his hands on the shine of it.

"Beautiful, man," he said.

"It totally is," I said and was glad I'd gone through the trouble, thought it looked real good, was yelling over Petty that I'd managed to snag a half-dozen bottles of Mad Dog 20/20 from my older brother's stash that he liked to keep hidden in a 12-inch drain pipe that ran under our parents' driveway. Feeling more alive than I'd felt all year, the bottles clanged in the trunk as we swung through the wide country turns of Route 71, three or four miles northeast of town, just shy of Starved Rock State Park.

To allow for yet another access road for a landfill that had been gutting property values all around Oglesby, the whorish county board had spent the past year tearing up soy fields and putting in those turns. My dad had told me that the Times said that it only took a week for this drunk guy, Chad Meyers, this future loser my brother knew, to already miss the curves coming home from a party at ISU. He had hit the ditch at full speed, upwards of 60 MPH in his rusted-thin Jimmy. He split his lip and the frame both in two when he left the blacktop, got launched into the air by the ditch and struck land again. The paper said that the back half of the Jimmy's frame and its wheels were embedded in the ditch, axle-deep. The front half was found almost twenty-five yards into the soy. Meyers, somehow totally alive, was wasted and had stumbled out of his seat and collapsed on the recently irrigated field. He had drunk and bled enough that, by the time the cops got to him, he was passed out facedown. They flipped him over and found that he had turned the mud ruddy and had an arching bruise from the wheel that rose like the sun from his collarbone to his jaw.

As Shawn and I drove by where all this had happened, there was still a huge gash in the soy. Like some long, dark runway, it compelled you to drive into it, follow it instead of the road and to whatever end, and the detail in the ditch seemed to be good enough that I pretended I could make out the manufacturer of Meyers' tires as I slowed to take the tail end of the curves.

I followed the directions Shawn was giving me beyond paved roads and into tar and chip, which then turned into two deeply packed grooves in the earth that eventually just gave way to a pair of battered tracks of dead grass that slithered ahead of the car, wagged the wheel. Erica's beat and dusty Cavalier sat in between a bunch of trees and was hidden from the view of the now fairly distant county road. I parked next to it. Knowing what I knew about her, which was almost nothing, I couldn't believe her car was actually there and that she'd come to meet up with us. But there she was, The Smiths swelling out her windows, waiting for us.

Erica was a year older than us and had a boyfriend. I knew it. Shawn knew it. Everyone knew it because he was a big bastard. I happened to grow up next to him, went to grade school with him, and he was always nice to me, but he was a big bastard to a lot of kids. He hung around with this Josh Soto, always hung around with Soto and Soto was a fucker, always was a fucker, didn't have one redeemable quality in his body. This is in no way hyperbole. Oglesby High School had been checking for something of value in Soto and they found nothing. They had sent him to office after office, psychological and otherwise, and then, seemingly exasperated, dealt with Soto by suspending him again and again until he, by this time in our lives, had already been blacklisted from the only two schools his poor parents had to choose from in the area. It never occurred to me that a person's children could render an entire region uninhabitable, but Soto proved it possible indeed.

Erica's boyfriend, though, Adam, while an asshole to most kids, was human enough but never bothered to come to class, so his high school career was already over too. He, in comparison to Soto, was taken down more traditionally, like a lot of people I knew: by his absentee parents' general lack of ability to assimilate into society in any meaningful way. I was on my way to a friend's growing up when I saw Adam's trailer being hauled away by a semi, Adam carrying boxes into a neighboring trailer. Even at nine I was scared for him. It's unlikely that you can really understand the context of such a thing happening at that age, but seeing someone's entire house being driven off and going down a frontage road is plenty concrete enough to burrow through the naiveté about the world you may have at any age.

That said, my thinking that my amicable past with Adam would hold sway over him may have given me some false confidence as the events of the day progressed. It was an afternoon that began nicely enough, just a stock Midwestern afternoon, a little wind, a little sun, some gnats, some smokes, but it went south in a hurry at a carnival later that evening, in such a hurry Adam didn't even have an opportunity to drop this bear he had won for Erica before he and Soto came down on me like a framing hammer.

But it was already over for me early on, because Erica was wearing this really hot blue two-piece, had her bare feet on the dash. I wasn't about to ask questions that needed to be asked to spare me. She looked amazing smacking the side of a swirled-glass bowl on her knee, grinding the base end of a lighter into it. She took a bit and handed it to someone lying in the backseat. This girl sat up, waved at us, and Shawn was giddily animated at the surprise of Katie Waltham, a friend of Erica's we both happened to know pretty well.

Shawn's initial interest in Katie, rather than his future wife, was obvious but likely a choice he'd made in deference to me. Since I'd shared how I felt about Erica earlier in the week when she walked past us in the hall at school, he knew I was into her. I thought he was being a good friend, and he was, but as it goes, he also just knew Katie better then. Shawn's trailer park was separated from Katie's neighborhood only by a thin line of hickories and about 200 yards of this partially developed dirt someone had purchased to turn into another, hopefully track-free neighborhood. But whoever bought it had only gotten as far as paving a small entrance and had managed nothing more in the five years they'd been working on it. But, besides having gone to Wallace Grade School with Shawn and I, Waltham had spent her youth forced into bands and choirs because of her deep love and subsequent ability to flat-out fucking wreck a piano, a talent that all the partying she had done since grade school had little to no effect on. Sitting like that in the back of Erica's car, surrounding herself in the dust of slinking smoke, you couldn't tell that she had the kind of talent and skill that would eventually have her playing for the Chicago Symphony Orchestra, but you could tell that there were these deep and barbed inroads of all the practice she must have put in to do well in such a pursuit, because she always – a piano being in the song that was on the radio or not – she always played a phantom piano on whatever object happened to be around. She was doing exactly that. I didn't know much, but because my brother was harassing his own musical fantasies at the time, I knew enough about music to notice that she was playing a left hand just like a real left hand should be played. Her being there also said a lot about who Erica was. She had quality friends.

Erica, meanwhile, had spent her youth in nearby Seneca right up until they closed her grade school and her family skipped their way downriver to Utica. Utica is this little two- or three-block township that got flattened by a tornado a few years back, but like one of the beautiful weeds, has since popped up again, all the prouder for having done so. I found Erica infinitely interesting. She read a ton for a kid from around there, had been places you couldn't get to by car, didn't seem all that interested in what I thought was cool about her, but I was certain that she would just be fun to be around, something she actually turned out to be, always game, the type of person I hoped I'd one day turn into but never did. Erica'd go on to survive the tornado that razed Utica. She would marry and bury Shawn, have kids with him, but that day, I was the kid. She was too. We all were and she was still possible for someone like me, at least just as possible as anything else.

Pipe in her mouth, Waltham's fingers tapped the back of Erica's seat and Erica had this seemingly permanent smile on her face. When Waltham handed the bowl back to her, Erica held onto Waltham's hand, kissed it. Waltham put her arms around Erica for a hug, and not being particularly lucky people, Shawn and I were thoroughly lost in the watching of the whole thing. Enthralled, we sat in our car like grade school boys, scared to move and ruin this exchange between the two. Being around a scene as beautiful and as sexy as that, and being the losers we were, we actually high-fived to our rare good fortune.

Erica and Waltham hopped out and we all tore off into a thin trail that slunk through the woods and to the falls, a bottle of 20/20 each, with Erica as our guide.

Nobody said much. We just followed one another, hurried toward the sound of tumbling water.

Erica had obviously been there before. We came out of the nest of trees and onto this butte. Erica, without even turning around, barely managed to drop her handful of things into a tuft of grass and weeds before she ran right off the end of the rock, her sunglasses still on. We all ran to the edge and watched her fall, hit the water, disappear. I began counting to gauge when I'd have to dive in and save her. My softheaded, archaically chivalric tendencies already had me taking off my pants, but pausing at the button. I was not quite brave enough yet to go full nude. Erica erupted from under the water and saved me instead. At some point, she had lost and then found her sunglasses again. She was waving them in her fist as she bobbed on the surface. Her chest and neck heaved. Even seventy feet below us, you could see how much she thoroughly enjoyed the jump. She was bursting with life down there.

Shawn leapt next, his shirt and pants still on, rolled to the knee. He hit the water hard and then Waltham, now naked from the waist up, slipped past me in a blur and over the edge. I watched her hit the water as well and, having listened to way too much Megadeth and N.W.A. over the course of my life to allow myself to chicken shit up there, I took off too.

Erica was so totally right to feel the way she did. I wasn't watching the approaching water as I fell the seventy feet at all. What I was watching was the grainy, exploding mass of dark green woodland and soft blue sky. It was a thrill, to say the least. Color was everywhere, sun punctuating everything like periods on a page, and time did not slow – a hokey fantasy – instead it all just happened non-linearly. Everything seemed to be happening at once and with an intensity that made me question nothing, rather than everything, which was what I thought would have been my impression. Nothing about that fall was fearful, but I could see how such an experience could be mistranslated as such if you weren't in the right place, the right mind.

I was in the right mind.

But deep under the milky, muddy water, I was certain that something hit my leg. I'm that guy anyway, but there was a rumor – there's always a rumor surrounding dive spots like this one. There was a rumor that the farmer who owned this land had gotten sick of kids coming and swimming there, was worried about insurance and whatnot, so he filled it with – not piranhas or electric eels or something, as that would be so obviously unbelievable that it would deter no one – no, this farmer filled our spot with loads of carp and catfish. The rumor was that it just made the experience super unpleasant, not deadly at all, and I was sure that I was feeling some of these so-called innocuous fish encircle me like tiger sharks and it was freaking me out.

The others were already halfway back up the hill to do it again, but I was stabbing my hands into the water to maybe feel what was really inside. Wearing myself out, I twisted around like a locked knob and was starting to feel as though I were in a massive washer, that I was being agitated to near-death levels. Waltham, displaying whatever the complete opposite of shy is, rumbled back down the hill and came over to the side of the waterhole as I slapped to the edge of it. Bent over, her breasts hung in front of her, and being naked seemed to bother her a lot less than I would have thought it would. Shattering my neat and naive notions of how a half-naked girl should act all over the place, she just reached out. I could smell the Aussie dripping from her hair as she pulled me out of the water.

"Christ," I said, saved. I was redefining excitement as I spoke. "Did you guys feel all those fish in there?"

"That's bullshit, man" she said, big smile on her face. "There's no fish. You imagined it. And those jeans? Take a look at yourself. They're fucked."

Midway along the left thigh, my jeans were torn down just to the two seams; they were no more. They were now a kind of shorts, and as soon as I finished the job and saw how easy it was to remove the leg completely, I realized how thinned and dried out the old jeans actually were. The other leg was ripping at the ankles and I completed the look while still on the shore. I was lucky they tore where they did. Any higher and there would have been problems/exposure. I kind of wanted it.

I soon got it.

The waterhole was fed by a shallow branch of the Illinois River, but the river itself, which was not shallow at all but wide and wild with churning currents, is miles away there. This left only a petering out, maybe a foot deep stream that spilled over a series of slippery rock shelves that, if you sat in them, were only just barely strong enough to occasionally move you from your spot.

Eventually, after we jumped a few more times, this was where Erica and I ended up. You could see Shawn and Waltham messing around on the butte. Flashes of their skin flared in the sun. Erica was watching. Shawn kept peeking at us over the edge. He was being obvious about it and Waltham, at some point, tossed Shawn's clothes into the waterhole as I cheered her on. Erica and I sat there. With yellow moss clinging to the rocks and wagging like streamers in the wind, we spread our arms along the edge of the shelves. The water poured over our shoulders and kept trying to strip Erica of her swimsuit. I prayed to a god I didn't believe in as she held it on, but the weight of the water was rushing over our bodies and it did eventually win. But, it was me who lost. Too fast to do anything about it, my jeans failed at the waist. The seam came apart like paper and all I had left on was a strap of denim material, now nothing more than a belt. The rest of my jeans slid down the rapids and into the waterhole, spun on the surface along with a couple Mad Dog empties.

Important things germane to personal self-esteem came together for me out there. Though reluctantly bare-assed, I didn't even bother to cover myself. I resisted the instinct and just stood up, flapped around in the sun for a second. I pretended as if my nakedness had no effect on me or others at all and then, when an entire body's worth of goosebumps consumed me, I turned around, popped the button on what was left of my jeans and plopped backward into the water, my arms up and out like some crucified Christ. I could hear Erica laughing while I was under the water, it filling my ears and working to muffle her out.

Shawn and Waltham had discovered me too by the time I had resurfaced and Shawn took it as an opportunity to jump in with me. His hand covering his crotch the whole way down, he almost hit me on his way in. I could feel water, his body rush past my legs. Then water filled my mouth and the taste of clay was strong. It cleared the Mad

Dog Banana Red and Camel Wides out straight away and replaced it with salty grit. I swallowed the cloudy gulp, while Shawn, simply ebullient, splashed around, gathered his soaked clothes.

If you've ever lost badly or were ganged up on in strip poker, you know that there's a point where you don't even care anymore that you're naked, assuming you ever did. This is growth. You acquire a kind of spousal confidence in your body, simply because other options aren't really available anymore. At least this kind of confidence should be the goal for you. Unless, when you find yourself exposed, you're the kind to cower, which is when those around you lose all respect.

I, however, at least in this way, if no other way, was the ideal. I strutted back to the car like a marital veteran coming back from the bathroom in the middle of the night. There were some scant plans to stop by the Peru Mall and pick me up Penney jeans, which we eventually did do, but since Erica wasn't recoiling from me in repulsion, I couldn't have given a shit if I ever wore pants again. I was feeling out and out Cro-Magnon, emboldened by the fact that Erica was still talking to me, walking beside me. That said, it was the first time I had experienced what is the bitless freedom of what I would now call monogamous nudity. Even though we weren't committed to each other in any real way, she treated my body like we were, like it was fully-clothed, and rather than feeling weird, it felt liberating. I had attained on our way back to the car, somewhat miraculously, that Waltham-level of comfort with my body. You could tell that there were no moves coming from Erica, but more importantly I didn't feel the need for any. At that moment, I was a teen god; no, just a god. I was so confident in myself that, out of knowledge that I knew I couldn't possibly manage to piss away the obvious currency of cool I'd just obtained, I let fly a yip like a puppy when I sat on the really hot hood for a smoke when we got back to the car.

We chitchatted about this and that for a while, reloaded on 20/20, and left.

We should never have been driving. Our two cars wavering around the wide lanes of country roads, to the mall for me, and then back into Oglesby as the sun fell away into the scorched fade of the horizon in our rearview, put God only knows how many people at risk. But we made it all the way back to Shawn's, totally fucked up, having managed to not hit and drag any people or any animals under our cars on the way.

His parents always gone, off to wherever – it never matters where at that age, so long as they're not around – we all kept it up, finished all but one of our bottles and I'll admit I whined a fair amount when Waltham told us that she and Erica would have to leave soon, meet up with us later.

Since it was when more people I knew had scanners than cell phones, a time when actual plans between people had to be made in advance, phone trees memorized, we designated the carnival on the north side of nearby Ottawa as the place where we'd meet up that night.

Shawn and I took what was left of our last bottle of Mad Dog down to Ottawa's Allen Park, taking back roads and caution. The evening air had brought out the bugs, was damp from late spring humidity. Some people who don't like the smell of rivers, which is to say that they don't like the smell of fish and rushing mud with a current, would say that the river stunk that night. When it's hot like it had been for days on end, those with enough money to have pools love that kind of weather because it warms their water for free, but the same can be said of a river, and Shawn and I had spent a lot of time in the Fox and Illinois that slam into one another in Ottawa. There's a current that spins under the bridge there, that takes you down if you let it, takes you under if you get careless and too close to the water that churns visibly. Like storm systems strong enough to produce tornadoes, the Fox mixes violently with the Illinois, and right where that happens is Allen Park. People have jumped from the bridge that joins Ottawa's north and south side and have died in that wash over the years. What killed those jumpers, people'd find out later, was not the fall – you can totally survive the fall – but usually their being towed under and slammed into what is a surprisingly rocky floor. The water's so active in that spot that it washes most everything away but the rock. The bed is hard like iron, like a skillet, and as part of a much more innocuous consequence, the rivers are noisy. Shawn and I went there with some regularity, sometimes just to listen to it, to smoke, skip, hang out, which is what we did that night. But as we pulled down the hill into the park, the air that slid over the river blew our lighters out, so we parked, rolled up our windows, lit our smokes, and trolled for fish bones and rocks smooth enough, flat enough to skip on the furrowing water.

Details are a bit foggy, but Shawn and I sat on a picnic table in this rain shelter that sits about twenty feet from the river, talked about the girls, and at one point, I was what I'd call numb drunk. I had been sitting on my hands, and only because I dragged them along the rough tabletop and cut them up a bit did I realize that I didn't really have much feeling in them anymore.

"You get anywhere?" Shawn said.

I figured it to mean about Erica, was right.

"Not yet," I said.

"Katie was into me," he said, "but we ran out of time."

"Who ran out of time?" I said. "You stopped it. You jumped off the thing and almost landed on me."

"Yeah, I guess so," he said. "She's cute, but I don't know."

"What?" I said. "Cute?"

Shawn smiled, took the bottle from me, fumbled off the table, off the concrete slab and fell in the grass. Devout, he held the bottle upright over his head and didn't spill a drop.

I got up and took it back from him, swigged from it.

"What?" I said again.

"Nothing," he said, now lying on his back, talking to the sky. "What about you two? Is that something?"

"I don't know," I said, and that was it.

Now, I wonder what he really wanted to ask me. I wonder if I was hurting him with all my trying for Erica.

Not much of anything happened out there except for that we ran out of liquor and had time to spend, so we spent it, got to talking. We were there for somewhere around an hour and a half. I only knew this because I noticed that it was the third time I had gotten up to launch a yawp over the river of "Hey, hey mama, said the way you move" from the first track of Shawn's Zeppelin album I had agreed to play for him. My voice was starting to hurt. I got up to change it when Shawn piped up.

"Zeppelin, dude," he said and flicked his cigarette into the river. "You got to sing it at my wedding someday."

He always said "dude."

I still do.

"I'm happy to sing at your wedding," I said, "but I don't get you with the Zeppelin."

"What is there to not get?" he said. "Bonham is really all you need to know."

"Lennon's all I need to know," I said (and still feel much the same way).

"Fuckin' Beatles," he said. "They ruin some good people."

Shawn was up and stumbling around in the grass now, getting closer to the sloppy river line, and seemed to have lost interest in skipping stones. He said "fuckin' Beatles" as he was tugging at a rock the size of a muskmelon that sucked as he pulled it from the ground. He lifted it with his hands, put it on his shoulder, then sagged backward toward me just before he launched the rock as if it were a shot put. Despite all the effort, Shawn made only a short toss. But following the rock in the air, I saw the lights from the football field at Marquette over the tall elm trees on the other side of the Illinois. Strange shaped clouds and then the dark infringed upon the edges of the light.

"Dude," I said.

Shawn was wiping the mud off his shirt, coughing, snapping his lighter on his jeans with the same action he always used to pack his Skoal: a quick up and down movement where the wheel of the lighter is used like a guitar pick – it's a move that is not dissimilar to what it looks like when people imitate the playing of that first, dual power chord from "Youth Gone Wild." This was a lighter trick he was better at – one he had practiced so much that all his pants had, to varying degrees, a couple-inch spot worn into them. You could tell how often he wore his pants by whether or not you could see his scraggly leg hair yet.

"Dude," I said again, thumbed over my shoulder, "let's go. They must be playing. It'll give us something to do."

Shawn squinted into the dark toward me and we eventually left, turned our radio down through the quiet streets of Ottawa's east side toward Marquette.

There's this abandoned area of Ottawa – well, abandoned by anyone who would be asshole enough to think that being middle class equates to being somehow better than, which if you're someone like me, seems to be true of a lot of people anywhere you go in America – but if you follow the Fox River north, away from Allen Park, there's a section of town that floods maybe once every ten years, but enough to run out anyone who can afford to run away. All the towns along the Fox, all the way to the northwestern suburbs of Chicago, and including Chicago itself, dump their storm water into that river. This often floods the more low-lying areas along the Fox all the way south. It doesn't stop in Ottawa, but the consequence of this is most felt in that particular area of town. Ottawa High School used to flood all the time as well but doesn't really anymore because, it being a school, the town taxed the shit out of people for a while and built a six-foot steel levee around the place. But for those who can't afford to do some private version of such a thing, or for some other stubborn reason I think I can understand, those who can't leave this periodically flooding area stick around and end up having to rebuild again and again. It's a generational thing. Some houses there have gone as far as doing what they do in more coastal areas: they gut the ground level and turn it into a permanently gaping garage or something. But, all this had made it so the neighborhood that Shawn and I were driving through seldom had any cops hanging around. It just wasn't well traveled and so, when we were drinking and driving or smoking and driving, we frequently would go through that area of town because we were relatively certain that the cops wouldn't catch us and they didn't that night either.

I put in Abbey Road, turned the radio up to Shawn rolling his eyes, and drove in circles for a bit so he'd have to hear my favorite songs from the record. As we got closer to the grounds surrounding Marquette, humidity was everywhere. My arm, which I had dangling on the door out the window, was gliding on the paint. My buzz waning but body clearly recovering, I pulled onto one of those makeshift, grass parking lots Marquette folks liked to use for their football games. Cars were nose-to-nose and door-to-door. Oftentimes there were coolers and lawn chairs that people just left out while they went in to watch their sons bash into one another, join their daughters in cheering it all on. All this was a habit which seemed to be some residue from the '50s, or at least my clichéd idea of what the '50s were like around there. Either way, some old ways still persisted then.

I see Ottawa differently now, more evolved than they were when I was young, but even by then my parents had gone from those who leave their doors unlocked to those who are beyond paranoid and seem to worry obsessively about some Capote-like demise. Like most places, the right amount of scared is somewhere in the middle, but a lot of people I knew had not quite settled on where exactly that middle was.

Anyway, Shawn and I got tickets, hot dogs, and ended up sitting on the Away side of the field for two reasons: 1. The Home side was always super packed. So unless you got there well before the game, there was very little chance that you'd get a decent seat and we weren't going to be able to that night either; 2. It being a Catholic school, we didn't give a fuck about Marquette beyond the fact that there were some girls that went there that we both were kind of into. There were some spots just onto the bleachers, spots people don't like because everyone is walking by and it makes it hard to see the game. But we weren't into the game, at least not football, so we sat down.

Shawn and I had a thing: We'd pretend to be in conversation with each other, and as someone walked by, we'd antagonize them in this overly aggressive way.

Consider this:

"Anyway," I said scanning the people passing in front of us for a potential victim as one approached, "I don't think much of – Go fuck yourself – Bonham, but if I ever said that Led Zeppelin sucked, then I think you could take issue with that."

The person I said "Go fuck yourself" to was a tall but still stringy kid with not much pop in him. You could just tell by his look that this was a kid that wasn't going to kick up anything and he didn't. But we warmed up quick.

"I could see that," Shawn said.

"I know you – Hey, fuck you – said that, but what do you really think?" I said as a more promising candidate strolled by, peering into the bleachers for a seat.

I could see on Shawn's face that this one had at least heard me and Shawn just tried to keep up the ruse.

"No," he said, "you're right all along. Ringo's always been the better drummer."

When he said that, I was certain that the ruse had been exposed.

The last guy was still behind me, a handful of his friends trailing him, and I could hear him asking them if they had heard what I said. From my periphery, I could see his friends bunching up and pushing him to keep him walking, which is what he did.

He was bigger, which was why I chose him – for the challenge of it all, I mean. But I thought that it was the last of him that I would see.

I was wrong.

As the game started up and Shawn and I bored of our own antics, we did that thing a few more times and let it taper off, actually watched some of the game. We got up and got some more dogs and I felt largely sober, but it seemed to me that Shawn was still pretty wily. He was leaning on snack shack walls and shit was falling out of his hands and mouth as he ate.

"You can see him up there," he said about our big target somewhere after halftime. "He still looks a little pissed."

We laughed it off, but I relished in the idea that my reasoning for poking at these people had paid off. I simply wanted to have an effect on some fellow loser's evening, and for all practical purposes, it was sure sounding like it had been a successful run.

The rest of the game came and went and the stands cleared all at once, flooded the parking area. Shawn and I weaved in between the noise of the people and packed-in cars. I followed the cherry of the smoke Shawn held over his head through it all, and when we made it to our car, Shawn swung around the back end to the passenger side and stopped suddenly, put his hands up.

On Shawn's side, the big guy that I'd provoked appeared out of the people, while two of his friends grabbed me from behind, took me by the shoulders, told me not to move.

I didn't.

What I did was watch as Shawn, too drunk and hapless to defend himself, got his ass handed to him by the guy I'd yelled at and a fourth guy that approached us slowly but had a fist up and ready. Shawn was already down before that fourth guy started in on him. All I could see from around my car were pistons of strikes and the hands of the two guys digging into the rooftop for balance when they began to kick him. Shawn had been talking at first, but as they backed away and were shouting at him, all I could hear was his coughing and what sounded like throwing up.

Once everything settled down, they said a bunch of shit, ran off, and left us out there.

The whole time I did nothing, forgot I was a wrestler, a friend, the instigator even. I was glad that it wasn't me getting beat on, really glad it wasn't me getting beat on. Who wouldn't be? But I watched it all and spent most of what was really only a furious minute of a fracas as a witness, but also watched scattering families shove their young kids into cars, tear off into the still new nighttime.

You know, those folks didn't know who we were, so it made me feel like they saw us as just some ugly disturbance and made me want to fuck around all the more. All told, we were some kind of unwelcome country import in their pleasant little place, but these very real distinctions between really country and almost country are totally lost on people that aren't from those places. Those little distinctions matter a lot, just fire you up, fiercely, and do so all the time. In a way, it's what made our game fun, sure, but also possible.

I could hear Shawn come to and some security dude screaming, coming at us, so I hurried around to Shawn, scooped him into the car, and we took off, sluiced around the lamplit streets, tried to stay low.

"You gonna make it?" I said.

He made a kind of sound that sounded like yes.

"Hey, hey, papa," I said and put on Zeppelin again, turned it up for him, decided I was plenty sober enough to not get a DUI, rolled the windows down in deference to his condition.

I took a marker out of the console and wrote on Abbey Road, "You'll love this someday. It's my gift to you to remember the night you got your ass kicked." I signed it and slid it into a pocket of his coat and forgot about it.

Shawn grinned when I gave it to him but was doubled over into himself like an arthritic fist. He was twisted in his seat, but never asked me why I didn't try and save him, never questioned why it was only him that took a beating. He eventually sat up and said that it wasn't the fight, but the 20/20 that held him back. He said that, if he hadn't been throwing up the whole time those assholes were beating the shit out of him, things may have turned out different and I actually kind of believed him.

But I got mine.

This battered Shawn and I showed up as promised at the carnival. I bought Shawn some soggy churros – I felt like I owed him more than just an old CD of mine that he didn't even like – and we wandered the grounds looking for Erica and Waltham, found them flirting with some carny rats flipping levers on an almost certainly poorly maintained deathtrap. If Shawn was able to be vertical, and if life was worth living at all, we believed that looking the way Shawn did had to be like candy for Waltham, and it was. She ran to him, pawed softly at his face and sat him down on the curb, kissed him.

"Who's responsible for that?" Erica said and didn't seem to expect an actual answer, never got one, didn't seem all that surprised by how Shawn looked.

Shawn's appearance was working wonders for him, but I had these hopes of scoring with Erica, so I told her that I wanted to go back to the car for something, and after we told Shawn and Waltham we'd be right back, we left.

On our way, my life took one of its better turns, at least initially. For some reason I never questioned, Erica came on to me and I fumbled around for my keys, stumbled into the backseat of my car, Erica's hands on my back, pushing me in.

I'd never been with a girl. That may not be surprising, but I didn't really get to be with one then either. I was so nervous and turned on that, as soon as Erica unbuttoned my pants and put a hand down them, it was all over. I knew that this was a sad performance, but it wasn't because Erica made me feel like it was. In the backseat of my car, what is a true kindness in her shone. I think she saw me for what I really was: a kid who was so disappointed that he still was one. I was deeply embarrassed, but she just eased back into the seat, helped me clean myself up and never stopped smiling at me. It's not going to be possible for me to explain how grateful I was and am for how she responded, but know that Erica ended up being one of the few girls I was ever with that was able to snuff out the terrible, inherent pressure of sex for me. I'll always love her for that.

Making our way back to the carnival, we met up with Shawn and Waltham, Shawn looking at us instead of Waltham as we approached. We went on some rides and we split up, separated from the girls for a while, and Shawn and I were heading back to the car when it was a giant, stuffed bear that I saw first.

Under Adam's arm was the biggest carnival prize you could possibly win. I was thinking about how much money and how long he must have spent at some tent in order to win the damn thing, but the dude looked downright heartbroken. This was a crestfallen man before me, Soto just behind him.

I'm not sure how Adam found out about Erica and me, but as he stood there shouting, bear under his arm and all, there was just enough wobble in his voice, that almost crying glimmer in his eyes, to be certain that he did. It didn't matter that what had happened in the car was just an awkward, adolescent thing. I knew I was going to be that outlet for violence that so often accompanies these kinds of situations and that's exactly what happened, and it happened fast.

Somewhere in the space between us, Adam swung at me, missed, and being a lot bigger than I was, he sort of smothered me like a huge blanket, and we fell to the ground as one awkward unit. He hit me softly a number of times along the side while we were in the gravel, shouted random shit in my ears, and then just got up, said what people say when they're trying to end a fight. The bear had somewhere squeezed out and I was lying on top of it. Adam was tugging its arm and I rolled off of it, uninjured in really any way. The whole fight was weirdly frenetic and I was dirty but fine. Adam had taken it easy on me.

I got on my feet and started to dust myself off, was bent over cleaning up the dirt on my new jeans when Soto chipped in.

"That's not how you hit a motherfucker," he said. "This is."

I didn't even see it coming. Soto hit me behind the ear and I did hear it, but everything went black.

When I came to, my head was resting on a parking block and I was in real pain. Blood ran off the end of my nose and rolled down the block, was collecting in a pile in the gravel. All things were hazy, but you could make out how it was Adam, not Shawn, mind you, but Adam who was holding Soto back. They twisted around together, tangled in that strange carnival light, then fled what was now a scene into the blurry glitz.

I suppose that I got what I deserved there and for a variety of reasons which are likely fairly clear to most, but when Shawn helped me off the ground, I was wavy, and one of my arms hung real heavy. The blood in my veins was almost audible, thrummed like a bass to the fingers, and I was having trouble making out what was what, so ended up saying, "Cotton candy."

I don't know why, but I wanted cotton candy badly.

I didn't get it.

What I got was help back to the car. Shawn, and somebody I didn't know, more or less hauled me there. They laid me across the back seat and I generally ached. Shawn took the keys, turned the car over, and the world through the back window swung quickly by. I found it nauseating, rolled over and threw up in the footwell behind the driver's.

"Dude," he said.

"We can't go?" I said.

I remember this as my wanting to go back to the carnival.

"Stop, dude. Stay still," he said and shuffled through the six CDs I had in my changer, none of which he let play for even one full song.

I sort of stopped, but my beating turned out not to be as bad as we had originally thought. I did feel way fucked up and, judging by the way Shawn was turning around in his seat and looking at me, I must have looked terrible. I know I did when I saw myself later, but as Ottawa's downtown flickered by behind him, Shawn's lively face beamed through his few new bruises settling in. I remember thinking that he looked vigorously happy.

But, we still took the Party O around until sometime into the night (this "Party O" I'm referring to is more or less a nine-block long, one-block wide strip of downtown Ottawa losers like us endlessly drove around). 'Course, what we would be praying for is for girls to notice what was, in our minds, how cool we looked in our cars, how aloof we could be and still pick up. But, due to the fact we would inevitably be blazing what were our arguably shitty tunes as loud as my Alpine would allow, it was more likely interpreted by girls as something more like we were asking whether or not they preferred the Spin Doctors, Pink Floyd, or The Doors. (Not surprisingly, we tended to score more favorable talks with the Spin Doctors since there's always that iffy crowd factor folded into anything involving Pink Floyd or The Doors which we had yet to pick up on.) This was where and when we came across Erica and Waltham again. I'd had my arm over my eyes in the backseat, was starting to feel generally better, when Shawn shouted at them out the window.

We stopped and Erica yanked open the door, slid the passenger seat forward and climbed on top of me.

I groaned at her.

"Oh, you're fine," she said, wound her face up, started looking around. "Dude, it smells terrible in here."

"I know," I said, pointed to the well. "Don't put your hand down there. You know, your guy, by the way – well, not your guy necessarily, but with fuckin' Soto, beat the shit out of me just after we saw you."

"I heard," she said with no real detectable pity or guilt.

There are these little folds of skin that I love under the arms of girls, with stubble and all. I love them and Erica's smelled real good. They were red and wet from the heat and all her likely running around, but they were right in front of my face. Somehow they still smelled like a distant musk, not like it was right next to me. I took a big breath of it. It hurt me to do it, but I took another. I winced under her.

"I can't believe that fucker," I said.

"You don't think you deserve it?" she said, put her hand under my shirt. The heat of her skin made mine feel cool.

"Oh, I probably did," I said and meant it, meant all the filthiness of it. "From Adam I did, yeah."

I smiled a little at her. She did too.

Shawn eyed us in the rearview.

When that tornado happened in Utica, it was my parents that sent me the link to the Daily Times page about it. Reading it, I thought of Erica, and Adam too, for the first time since the story I'm telling here had taken place. After high school, Erica, perhaps not surprisingly, had gotten back together with Adam. They had actually gotten married and disappeared. I wasn't looking, but I lost complete track of her. I couldn't tell you if she ever even graduated. Honestly, I wasn't trying to keep her on the radar anyway, but when I saw Adam's name in that article about the tornado, after the bar they'd been drinking in had fallen on them and killed Adam, I wasn't surprised. But the collapse had pinned Erica beneath the table they were sitting at near the front door and window. Through some stroke of luck, she had survived because of this additional structural support that apparently surrounds doors and windows. She was cut up and battered, but otherwise okay. Adam, though, only a few feet from her when he died, was crushed beneath a few stories of century-old brick for God knows how long – days, it turned out; it took days to recover Adam and all the other bodies from the bar. I didn't think about it much at the time, how much Erica must have been hurting having survived such a thing, having suffered the loss she had. It took a minute of sitting there at the computer reading the story, but it was the way Erica smelled that I remembered first. I finished the article before I ever remembered the rest of the day the four of us had, but it said that Erica had been pulled out of the rubble by a couple that lived in this tiny white house nearby. For a minute there, staring into that whiteout fizz of Hotmail's backdrop, I even let myself imagine that I probably would have been able to find her in that fallen bar because of Erica's lying on me in the back of my car. Even that pain I selfishly recast to spotlight me, thinking I could've rooted around in the rubble like a great dog.

It was Shawn that got together with her a couple years after the tornado. I never heard the whole story, but because my parents read the Times religiously, my mom had told me that she'd seen that Erica had gotten married again, this time to Shawn. The Times did this redemption story about her. I thought it was corny when my mom relayed the story, ignored most of the details, focused instead on Mom somehow remembering both Shawn and Erica's names, even though Mom frequently called me by the dog's.

In the backseat, Erica kissed me and pulled away, snuck a J in my mouth like sleight of hand, lit it, held the fire over me. Damn thing was just right, just what I needed.

Waltham dangled a sixer inside the window, started kissing the cans, pretended to play some kind of melody on one.

"Come back to the house?" she said.

"Where'd you get that?" Shawn said.

"Some guys," Erica said.

"Sure, some guys," I said. "Whatever. I don't even want to know. Let's go."

Shawn snatched at the beer and Waltham whipped it away as Erica helped me out the backseat, kissed me again. The girls ran back to her car and Shawn drove the two of us out of Ottawa, toward Waltham's.

71 was as dark as always and the headlights dissolved into nothing just inches from the road. The night sky was a solid navy, like looking down into the bottom of the sea. It was dark enough out there in the way out country that Erica's taillights shaded the sky slightly red every time she hit the brakes, and she was hitting them a lot. She would put some distance between us, and as Shawn began to close it, she'd slow down to like 20 or 30, give it gas and do it all again just to fuck with us. Through Erica's back window, Waltham kept pretending like she was going to flash us, moon us, didn't get around to it, and as we came to those turns that Meyers had missed, Erica missed them too. She fired like a rifle shot straight off the road.

I hit the dash when Shawn stomped the brakes, flung my car to the cusp of the ditch. Erica's taillights went out as the rear end of her Cavalier smacked the edge of the field hard, her headlights dragging and curling inside the dark of the sky like those searchlights they use to call superheroes. The car battered its way well into the field, bobbed like on the chop of an ocean, water skidding out behind it. Soy exploded into the air.

We leaned forward in our seats, only able to watch at first.

But it was quickly very quiet. Though their radio was still on, it sounded like it was way off somewhere, across something desolate and deep, more like the sound was crossing time instead of space.

Shawn got out first. I would have thought that I'd run to the car, this now just dumb, steel box that had somehow shut itself off, but both of us approached very slowly. It seemed to actually take a while to get to them, which is perhaps an obvious thing to say, but is nevertheless an accurate depiction. My shoes were sinking more the quicker I went, and I was thinking how lucky they were that her car had stayed on its wheels.

Shawn ran to Erica's side and found her crumpled up between the wheel and the seat, reached through what was now just a bunch of open spaces where windows used to be, touched Erica on an eerily crooked, fractured leg, and found it leaking black blood in the dark. I got to the car just in time to see her, sequined in glass, come to and scream out.

"We're going to get you help, Erica," Shawn said. He was amazingly calm. Every one of his movements was deliberate and alive.

Waltham, pinned upright between the driver's and backseat, was out. She was cut up and her head hung awkwardly to the side, but I remember finding her hands somehow miraculously unscathed.

There's something that happens to us. It's an instinct to shake that which isn't moving that consumes us in a moment like that, a moment when you're not convinced it will do anything at all. That instinct consumed me too.

I shook and shook Waltham, but she wouldn't come to. The skin around her eyes was already blackened and I pulled at it. I forced her thick eyelid open. From the blood on the roof, it seemed as though she'd hit it, and even though her eye looked like a black sun going down on the red surface of Mars, I blew into it, shouted in her face, but she remained unresponsive.

"Dude," Shawn said as I already started walking away.

"I'm staying," he said as I left.

Behind me, Erica huffing wildly, Shawn was trying to talk her down as I ran to my car, turned it over, took off, the back of it drifting in the grass, grabbing at the blacktop.

I pulled up to this farmhouse. I left the car running, open, music spilling out, and went right through the front door, ran straight for the phone. When this guy showed up with a baseball bat on the stairs, I held my hands up and told him what had happened while the police droned in the receiver, sent an ambulance out. Seemingly mostly stunned to see me in his kitchen in the middle of the night, his bat still waiting for a pitch, dude barely said a word except when he asked me if I had what I needed. He waited for me to hang up and start for the door again before telling me to hurry on out. I barely made it back outside before I could hear sirens wobble in the air, see them color the sky wild above the fields. It is my firm belief that never before or since had ambulances ever come so quickly in LaSalle County.

Looking the way I did, and since I knew Erica's car had a bunch of beer and probably weed in it, I drove right past the accident, everyone still out there, scared and screaming again in the field. A trooper with an ambulance in tow skimmed by me. I pulled over to the side of the road and turned to watch them stop at the edge of the ditch, throw a spot on Erica's car, make their way out to the scene.

You could hear Shawn yelling at them, but the trooper pulled him away from the car.

I wasn't going back out there no matter what. But Shawn stood in the mud of the field like a parent. I watched for a minute until a couple more troopers showed up, started setting down flares, and moved Shawn even further away from the scene and into the road, now only maybe ten yards away from where I was.

He backed toward me, still focused on Erica's car.

"She's out. They got Erica out," he said as they set her on a gurney. "She's going to be okay. I think she's okay."

"She is," I said, but had no idea.

"Jesus Christ," he said. "Is Erica going to be okay?"

"I think so," I said. "but I don't think we should be here."

"I'm not leaving," he said.

"I know," I said, and when Waltham got helped out of the car too, was able to stand on her own, I took off, Shawn never even once turning my way.

That day and long night, eternal now, who we were in high school fixed in each other's minds, had me typing twenty years later I already miss you, buddy under a picture of Shawn and one of his and Erica's kids on Facebook. He's sitting by the Chicago River on St. Patrick's Day, a blotchy, red baby on his lap. The water is a saturated cartoon green. The two of them are wearing these ridiculous Mickey Mouse ears made to look like two huge shamrocks.

I flipped through a lot of pics of Erica and Shawn, their family, really most of what he had on Facebook. As I skimmed through and saw the last pictures of him in the hospital, trying to hide tubes behind his back as he hugged his kids, I was overwhelmed by the cold knowledge that Shawn wasn't readying for a divorce at all, of course, but readying for cancer to get him. I started to leave something more on his page, something more personal, but stopped. I ended up just leaning back in my chair and keeping that day with him and Erica in my mind as long as I could, replayed that day where Shawn lives over and over again, and cried.

Then I wrote Erica back. I told her that I was thinking about him, and likely because I had not sung at their wedding, hadn't been part of their world at all in two decades, didn't go to the hospital that was only an hour away, the funeral home which was even closer, and probably because she thought I didn't want to be bothered with any of this anyway, she wrote a quick reply: "Address?"

It's a shock when you get older and really are surprised by how much you care about the death of someone you haven't talked to in years. All I wanted to do was to keep talking about Shawn with someone, with anyone, but was never more alone in my apartment than I was just then.

I gave Erica my address, and for the next few days, I obsessed about what it actually was I had thought that Shawn had given up on. Then, it occurred to me that it seemed like it was most everything I still am, that what he'd given up on is being friends with that. For most of my life, prior to hearing about Shawn dying, I would have taken pride in such a thing, but I really didn't anymore, and it hurt to know that he probably never did. I felt as low as I'd felt in a while, then picked up some 20/20, drove down to the Fox and Illinois, and had a smoke while Zeppelin howled from my car, wonderfully through the noisy wind off the rivers.

JOINING

The first time I was arrested was in high school. I was with Paul Lynn, this guy who moved to Portland to be born again, which meant, once I found that out, he was as good as dead to me. When I think about him now, how I like to see him is stoned, or maybe even mountain biking too fast along the same Oregon paths Prefontaine used to run on, instead of praising some Jesus. But in between classes, the morning before my arrest, I told Lynn that I had decided I could not bring myself to finish school that day. I couldn't bear Vern Culver's history intro class again, and Lynn's suggestion was that we skip, go camping. It sounded good to me, and we got terrifically high straddling these dormers that rose from the roof outside Lynn's bedroom, both of us wearing his dad's super expensive cologne in case we somehow ran into girls. For us it was DJ Magic Mike and not Live, or something else like that, that burst out the windows like a heavy smoke. I feel like I remember the curtains being pushed out the house from the inside and surging to the beat, like on waves of sound, rather than any soft wind.

Somewhere along the line, Lynn called Nasty Matt DiNona to pick us up and drive us all around, because Lynn's pet '72 Chevy Nova had a carburetor problem (and by "problem," I mean, we lit the carburetor on fire with a lighter fucking around with it in the dark the night before). When Nasty, this random guy Lynn knew from somewhere but who was a stranger to me, came to pick us up, I threw on Lynn's Harley T-shirt and his dad's white cutoff jean shorts for some reason I wish I knew and now wish I could totally take back.

But eventually we all took off. The three of us drove way out to this small patch of land that I only knew of as some property Lynn's dad owned in the woods along the Illinois River, a couple miles west of Ottawa, Illinois. We were all chain-smoking our way around in Nasty's fucked-up, matte-finished, light-brown Dodge that looked vaguely like some '80s police cruiser. This time it was Dr. Dre that shook the windows, pissed off some old guy mowing his lawn when we stopped at a light. We all laughed wholeheartedly at that guy, let smoke leak out our mouths like Snoop.

When we got to the property, we found it overrun with weeds, these little wavering sapling trees, and buzzing with so many bugs it forced our mouths shut. It smelled the way it used to smell when I would crush dandelions in my fist as a kid, smear them on my jeans, put the pulp in my pockets. When I looked at him, Lynn seemed embarrassed, like he thought it would be more or less ready to go for us, and Nasty and I watched him damn near hurt his shit trying to pull a whip of a tree out of the ground with just his hands. Nasty choked out cigarette smoke as he laughed, sitting on the hood of his car. Drawn to the curling smoke that rose like loose strings from the cigarette between his fingers, Nasty's knuckles, bent over the wheel, were so dry they cracked like abandoned cooking grease. But we all took a shot at that little tree eventually, both of us trying to make Lynn look weak, I'm sure. We all failed, and then the three of us drove undeterred across town to Farm and Fleet to buy some machetes in order to clear out a little space for a campsite. This was a thing that, at the time, seemed somehow totally logical.

Even though we were all teenagers, we ended up buying the machetes without any trouble and began to head back to the property when we saw Erin Lansky on our way.

Lansky was the older sister of this girl we all knew from our class. We all knew her, but I had been to her house. I had awkwardly made out with her younger sister, Marta, with this bizarre I, Madman movie I'd brought over (a movie I still love) playing in the background. After multiple attempts at trying to somehow see her naked, I got nowhere, and when I'd gone to use the bathroom before I headed home, I noticed that there were pictures of both her and her sister that hung on the wall. I liked how, in a way, they had to watch me go. I looked them right in the eyes as I went. Then, with my pants still down, I masturbated into the Lansky family toilet. Their watching me also made me make the hostile decision not to wash my hands.

But Erin Lansky had graduated a year before, had a certain something. That something was that she was gorgeous, much better looking than her sister, and we sped up alongside her car on the road, our radio still on and blaring, all our hair blowing around in the wind like loose silk on corn. I hollered out my window at her from the backseat, tried to get her to slow down, pull over, and

she actually did. I really couldn't believe it when she came
to a stop in the fire lane in front of Kroger's.

When we got up next to her, so the sides of our cars
almost touched, Lynn turned Dre down, and we all asked
Lansky what she was doing and whatnot, chatted her up.
Nasty was shouting over the both of us so loud that I could
actually feel his voice shaking the insides of my ears. He
was yelling about how we were having some party,
something we hadn't at all discussed, but sure as shit
would, should we be able to line up a girl as hot as Lansky.
Nasty was out of his driver's seat and sitting on the top of
his door so that the rubber sill seemed to split his thighs
like twine around a roast. I was trying to get him to stop
rapping his knuckles, to stop slapping the palms of his
hands on the rooftop, when I heard honking coming from
behind us. I turned around and saw a shitty blue car with
an impenetrable and bubbling dark tint on the windshield.
I simply stuck my arm out the window, gestured what I
thought was nicely for the car to go around, actually said,
"Go around," out loud to myself, and went back to
concentrating on the careful wooing of Erin Lansky. I lifted
my shirt to my nose to make sure I had put enough cologne
on. I had.

When the shitty blue car behind us began to honk
again, Nasty really piped up even more but was now
directing it at the car. He started shouting quite a bit at
them until he fell back down in his seat, pounded wildly
on the wheel. It was maybe two in the afternoon and the
whole parking lot was totally empty – totally empty. I
knew without a doubt the people in that shitty blue car
could've easily gone around us if they'd wanted to.

But, they didn't. What they did was honk yet again, and even though I was more demonstrative the second time around, I still, pretty nicely, tried to point out how much room they had with my hand out the window.

I did say, "Fuckin' go around," but I said it to myself. I more mouthed the words through the dirty back window of Nasty's Dodge.

But the shitty blue car honked again.

This time, I wasn't nice at all. I was out the window, clapping my hands for some reason and waving them around like the asshole I probably really was at the time, no matter what I say here.

But, honestly, we were all pretty pissed. I mean, Christ, even the beautiful Erin Lansky turned around and gave them the finger.

And then the shitty blue car honked again and it all went off.

Lynn fucking flipped out. He scuttled between the two cars and I watched him from the back window holding his machete all high. Then he lunged at the shitty blue car. He kicked at it like people do in the movies when a dog is humping their leg. He started kicking the bumper, and left long, wide patches of black rubber from his shoes behind, and the shitty blue car backed up and started to pull around us.

Through most of it I was fumbling around, trying to open the box my machete came in. But I got it open, and just as the shitty blue car got around us and slammed on the gas, filled Nasty's Dodge with the stench of their exhaust, I reached out the back window with my machete, held it as high as I could, and waved it around like I was charging into medieval war. A thin plastic protective bag was still taped to it and snapped in the wind like some cheap guidon. And when the bag ripped off, blew away, I watched it skip along the asphalt of the still totally empty parking lot as the shitty blue car tore off into the street.

Lynn shimmied fast past my window again and got back in, slammed his door shut and was laughing, laughing like a crazy person.

We all were. At least, we all were until Nasty took off after them. Lynn and I were both on board for quite a while, and we were all yukking heartily. There's no other word for it: what we were doing was yukking.

Eventually, I told Nasty that I didn't want to get into car chase kind of trouble, but he hurled us out of the parking lot anyway, and I watched from the rear window as the beautiful Erin Lansky, still shaking her head in park in the fire lane, swung out of view as we rounded the corner of the empty Hardee's drive-through that Nasty was using to head off the other car. He got slowed up by something and couldn't get to them in time, and the shitty blue car sped off, farther and farther away, deep into a quiet, bystanding Ottawa, and out of sight.

Nasty drove for a while where he thought that shitty blue car might still be, until Lynn finally came around and told Nasty that we should probably end chase.

Nasty looked downright maniacal. He was beaming. He was sucking his lower lip so hard I could see how each one of his teeth forced the blood from his lips, left white impressions when he started to yell at us. And even though he clearly didn't agree with either of us, to his credit, Nasty caved when Lynn started in on him. One thing I remember thinking was, even Nasty caves.

Just drifting quietly along the mid-afternoon streets of Ottawa, we began to make our way back to Lynn's house when he told Nasty to pull off into Allen Park. He pulled onto this long drive that leads from the road down to the river there. Lynn was saying that he wanted to stop and say hi to his dad, who was on the river with his boat and a couple of guys, fishing. Lynn's dad didn't seem all that surprised, or even angry, to see the three of us there on a school day. Instead, when he saw us, Lynn's dad slipped the boat across the water and to the shore, cut the motor, coasted along the river line. His friends ignored us, drank. There was this slapping of river water along the wooden side of the boat and I could hear cars passing on the street behind us. We all chatted for a while about this and that, and eventually, we got back into our car and left Allen Park to head back up to Lynn's, which was maybe a thirty-second drive, seven blocks away.

The street that led into Lynn's neighborhood curved up a hill and everything up there was somehow oppressively tree-lined and always seemed downright too residential for someone like me.

But, we never made it to Lynn's place. We got up the hill and only a few blocks before Lynn's house, a cop car pulled out from one of the side streets, stopped right in front of us. Nasty jerked the wheel quick and made like he was going to turn down another street, but found it, too, stopped up by a second cop car, its silent lights whirling like the club. I suppose it's probable that there was sound, but I couldn't hear it, and when Nasty saw that second car, he did give in. He came to a stop, put it in park, laid his hands on the dash. Another couple of cop cars showed up and pinned us in. They started in with the megaphone, told us to get out.

I was shaking. I'll say it was because I was excited, but in reality, I was probably a little scared. There was this cop that was hiding behind his cruiser door like he would if it were in some movie, some Lethal Weapon or something, or like he actually believed us to be truly dangerous, murderous. And without waiting for Lynn and Nasty, I got out, and did so quickly, even though I was told to do so slowly.

When everything kind of settled down, Lynn and I had both ended up with our hands on the roof of the car. Nasty was cuffed to his own grille and looked a little pathetic, almost used to it all. But I was there just praying that someone at Jennifer Laurie's house wasn't home to see me like that: hands across a Dodge, cops everywhere, steps from her door.

Laurie was this girl I'd always had a crush on since I first met her my freshman year. I knew she was at school. I was pretty sure that her mom was too, her mom being a teacher there. Laurie didn't even know where her dad was anymore, so he was a non-factor to me. But I can tell you this: I liked that girl enough to have a pretty good idea where she was during school hours—it was first-hour algebra with Wallace, second-hour gym with Dalton, etc. She was a year older than I was, and when I first met her, she looked like how you'd think she'd look if I just told you that she was some Hollywood version of a curly-haired, blonde Midwestern girl. But to be fair to Hollywood, that's both a cliché and a thing. I asked this Will Caston guy about her, got her number that way. That's just how she was. She was the kind of girl you ask about, and eventually, I ended up dating her for a little more than a year. But that was before she went to college and long, long after I had my hands on the roof of Nasty's Dodge in front of her house. I don't think she ever found out about what would be my arrest. I know I never told her and she never said shit to me.

But Nasty, still cuffed to his car, was revving up again and started shouting, spit at one of the cops. He was pointing at the whole bunch of them, calling them creative things, things that had nothing to do with their profession, or really, even what they looked like, or the situation in general; it was just mad shit. But the cops got him to stop by one of them coming over and standing right in front of him. Guy didn't even say a word, didn't touch him, stood there staring at Nasty. The guy's nose was so red that, even from some distance, you could see that nest of small veins drunks get. Another cop approached me and asked if I had any weapons in the car, and I, since I was who I was, said yes. Unaccustomed to being a criminal, I was genuinely trying to help the man – naively, I suppose. I took my hands off the roof and began to reach inside the car. This, of course, turned out to be the wrong answer. As the cop grabbed me and jerked me around by the back of my shirt, I could hear threads tearing. He slammed me down by the neck on the trunk lid, told me to stay where I was.

I did.

Lynn, as I saw him then with my cheek pressed against the hot trunk, looked – well, scared. This surprised me. I had seen him as something else before that moment, and I was a little charmed by it, this new vulnerability. In our little group, I guess I felt like I was that guy up to then, the more scared-shitless type. But seeing him like that, we switched out there. I closed that off, got my shit together. I didn't want the cops to see that I was rattled. I didn't want anybody to see that I was rattled. But Lynn was sweating, and his eyes were actually glassy. I could see the tendons and the little muscles of his hands flexing, his fingertips digging into the roof of the car. But I was manually shutting down.

As soon as the cops gathered us all up and we were brought to the station, they separated us. They sat me at a table in this one room, Lynn in another, and what turned out to be the last time I ever saw Nasty, two cops were leading him down some hallway, his edgy-drifter button-down untucked, his hands in fists behind his back.

I had been in the room where they put me once before. My cousin had gotten sideswiped by a car pulling out into the street unannounced. The car was fucked. My cousin was fine. My aunt and uncle had been out of town, and I went with my parents to pick my shaken cousin up. We all sat in that same room, and there I was again, sitting there with no one to talk to. There was this one cop who was apparently there to watch me should I do something crazy, something I granted him since I had been brought in on machete charges. But he wasn't really there. He sat there, silent, vacillating between staring at the door and the clock on the wall until an older cop showed, pulled up a chair next to me and took out a small pad of paper from his chest pocket. He set it down on the table and looked up at me. He didn't say anything for a second.

There was a fruitcake in the middle of the table. I shit you not. It must have been left behind from some cop celebration because it was half-eaten. A piece of it had flopped over on top of the butter knife still there.

"Let's just get that away from you," the cop said.

He reached for the knife, smirking at his joke, and pushed it along the table, out of my reach, started in on getting me to give him a statement.

I took my time telling him what happened. I tried to be honest. I told him, in quite a bit of detail, how the people in the shitty blue car had fucked with us, how they kept honking at us, that we just wanted to scare them a little bit, wanted them to fuck off and go away so we could talk to a girl I didn't name. I tried to give some ground and admit that it got way out of hand, that we tried to tell Nasty not to follow them, that Lynn and I both had, and that I wasn't sure why it was such a big fucking deal. It all seemed plausible to me. I was telling the cop all this when he told me that the people in the shitty blue car had somehow gotten behind us, followed us to the park, and called the police from a pay phone. He told me that's how the police had intercepted us on our way back to Lynn's so easily. I started in saying that we wouldn't have actually done anything with the machetes, and then the cop asked how the two women with a baby in the car could have known that, and I stopped talking.

He led me out of the room and I saw two women sitting on a bench in the waiting area of the lobby, one of them holding this baby. They stood up when I walked out, started in on me, were shouting over my trying to apologize to them. I ended up standing there, saying as little as possible, and just took it. Last thing I said to them after they settled down was that I was sorry. I guess I was.

I remember this all as though I was charged, although my parents told me later that, since I was just a kid, I wasn't. But after I was put back in the room where I was questioned, they came in and told me to call someone to come and pick me up. I called my cousin. I didn't know if the cops would let me go with him, but they did. I called him because I was pretty sure he wouldn't say shit to my parents. I was holding out hope on my way home, was downright optimistic that I could deal with it all on my own without my parents ever finding out.

They found out.

However, the night before they did, my dad was sitting at the kitchen table with the Daily Times, my mom stirring up something in a huge pot on the stove. My dad read out loud from the paper how these two sixteen-year-olds, who he was calling "assholes," and some eighteen-year-old named Matthew DiNona, the only one of us old enough to actually be named in the paper, who my dad referred to as a "punk," had gotten arrested. I remember wishing I would have been referred to as a "punk." He read that these two "assholes" and a "punk" had gotten arrested for threatening a carload of two women and a baby in the parking lot of Kroger's grocery with machetes. My mom shook her head in disgust, set her wooden spoon down on those little aluminum things people set wooden spoons down on, and got bowls out of the cupboard. My dad asked the room in general how stupid someone had to be to do something like that. I sat there quietly, waited to be served my dinner.

My dad found out the next day at work. One of his coworkers at Libbey-Owens-Ford had a daughter that knew Lynn and me, and as it turned out, Lynn had been telling a bunch of people at school, like the dickhead he was, what had happened. My dad put it together rather easily, and when I came home from the school the following afternoon, he took my stack of CDs and the keys I was carrying away from me, and in a mad rage, but somehow still in one kinetic and furious move, my dad threw my stack of shit deep into the woods behind our house and then told me to go pick it all up.

I spent the next I don't know how many weeks out behind the house searching for what turned out to be shards of miscellaneous media and a rusty Corona keychain bottle opener. And when somebody somewhere figured out what to do with us, Lynn and I ended up cleaning the six empty cells in Ottawa's tiny police station as a kind of punishment. While we were doing it, we started up with songs from Grease – you know, "Greased Lightning," do-be-doobie-do-wop, and all that. The cops cut in on us over the intercom, told us that we'd be thrown in one of the cells if we didn't knock it off, and over a few weekends that began our summer that year, we scrubbed all the walls, cleaned all seven of the town's cop cars, painted the station's garage floor gray again, until, because of the fumes, they let us sit out in front of the station, and we laughed it all off, sang out there.

In the end, my parents told me that, years after I stopped hanging out with him, Lynn was born again. I saw this galvanizing stand-up bit where Dennis Miller says about the goofy religious act, "Excuse me for getting it right the first time," and I never even really considered such a ridiculous thing. But in a weak moment one afternoon my junior year, I did drive to Peru, Illinois, where I proved that I could do twenty-five push-ups without dropping to my knees to some jackass recruiter, and joined the Army, the perfect place for me.

ORIGIN STORIES

We're in Chicago. It's my first time here. I'm 14. It's '89. July. We're at Field's. Your J (who is of course Aunt J to me) and I are on an escalator. A yellow beam of sunlight drags across her. Pearl buttons flicker. The escalator hauls us out of this heat outside. Hitting the air conditioning's a rescue, but it's the year both you and Dad die: Dad's heart on the lawn, mowing; you on a plane in Iowa.

"You look pretty today," J says.

I don't say anything.

A white wall passes behind J like a blank sky. She puts her hand through her hair, then flutters her fingers out in front of her as loose strands fall. She's casting a spell. I think it's a sexy thing to do.

J tries a new angle.

"How are you and your mom getting along?" she says.

I don't say anything about how bad it's been between Mom and I, about the distance, the abuse, but my silence is enough here too. She knows exactly how it's been and probably doesn't really want to hear more bad news about her sister.

"You can say anything to me," she says. Her face tells me she knows I think she sounds like a fucking movie.

"I know," I say anyway.

This blurry heat off the street bends images outside. Out there, everything sags in carnival grotesqueness. But in Field's, J and I are in this deeply '80s glitz of the young men's department. It's Chicago, so I guess it has to be Bulls jerseys, Pippen and Jordan everywhere. Duran Duran's staring at nothing in this video that's playing on a huge bank of televisions.

It's "Notorious," the video. It's a pop-perfect Simon Le Bon, then a barren landscape. It's countryside on fire. Staring at the TV, I can smell the smoke, burning wheat. There's flashes of landscape in these almost obstreperous black and white shots, and then it's Le Bon again. This obvious object of a woman, whose age I envy, dances in slow motion in a blood red dress.

We're killing time, waiting for you. We're meeting you at that restaurant you guys like across town, some Gene and Georgetti's. The whole thing is you and J's tradition for when you come back from those business things in Denver.

Everyone always knows when these trips begin and end. When one of them's going on, no one can ask J to do anything. Everybody hates that. The whole family talks behind your backs about how much they can't stand how J arranges her life around your trips. Mom's forever saying she doesn't like it, but Mom doesn't seem to like anything after Dad. I interpret everything she does as her liking me even less.

I sometimes hold it against J, too, how much she gives you, but she keeps at her watch.

In secret, I love that you guys make that much effort for each other, and I'd never been downtown, so I asked to come. I had lied to J and told her that Mom said I could come up with her. J trusted me, but I'm loitering in spaces. I'm trying to be lost, left behind.

In a sea of silly, red paraphernalia, J stands alone. Off-gases of carpet and polyester clothes choke the air. J waves off some salesperson. She's smiling in front of the TVs, at Simon Le Bon, touches him.

She looks pretty standing there, her hand on the TV, kinked at the hip. And you're right, J looks a lot like Elizabeth Bishop, this poet you always loved.

Bishop would become my favorite poet too, but you show her to me, the back of her book in your den years earlier, when I'm just a kid. Bishop's sitting on brownstone steps in a New York in monochrome. The sun comes through the blinds, over your shoulders. It lays bright ribbons on the floor.

"She looks exactly like her," you say. "Look at her."

"She does," I say because I can tell how much you want me to confirm it.

You look past me, into the kitchen, call J in. I can smell ham in the oven, dumplings in a Crock-Pot. Family chatters everywhere. To me then, it's all just noise settling like silt. J comes in, takes one look at the book in your hands and walks back out, but you're right. She looks a lot like Bishop. She really does when she smiles.

Partly through reading the intro out loud to me in your den, I look up at you and you take the book, fold some pages over, tell me to read it later. Swirling, dusty light warms the carpet.

I do take the book home, but it's only way later, after I'm grown up and both you and Mom are gone that I actually read all the poems you dog-ear. I even take the lonely book with me when I leave for ISU, but it just sits on a shelf like books do. It's some dull kid at a party, surrounded by so many brighter stars. It's there with Middlemarch, with Proust, with Infinite Jest, all books I buy because people think I'm smart. Even though I eventually do read the things, it's really more a matter of my being just smart enough to know what I should display.

I want you to know that I did finally realize that all the poems you marked for me are about abuse, that you knew then what I was going through, were trying to be helpful. It turns out you were too subtle for a thick, young version of me. And when I finally realize what you did for me, you're gone and I can't call you and thank you for being the first person to try and help me. Unlike I'm doing now, I can't tell you while you're still alive that I forgive you for not trying to do more, so I tear the pages out, put them in a drawer. I cry, alone in my apartment.

But in Field's, J hums softly to herself.

"Oh my god. There he is," J says like a girl I wouldn't like. "What's the matter with me? I love him."

She laughs and it's really good. Her mouth's the length of a subway wall, all teeth, all Bishop. I'm obsessed with J's smile, how big her mouth is. It's wide open. She has one hand trying to cover it.

"I know," I say, smile at Le Bon too. I can kind of see the appeal. I look around the store for guys who share any feature of his tabloid juvenilia. "You're not alone. All my friends like him."

"He always reminds me of your uncle," she says. "It's unbelievable. Am I imagining it?"

She is. I lie.

"Totally," I say.

I picture you on the screen: you, then girl in red dress, then burning countryside; you, red dress, black and white Le Bon, scorched country. It doesn't work.

We're on pause together. More people dribble off the escalator. This big guy looks me right in the eyes, puts his arm around his kid's shoulder. I watch them walk off into everything until they're gone. The kid looks back at me as he disappears. I wave, ultimately to no one.

The air conditioner whirs, dumps cold air on us.

"When's his flight get in?" I say. J shoves things she'd never buy around on racks. The hangers squeal.

"Soon," she says, checks her watch again. "God, it's freezing in here."

"Okay," I say.

I take her wrist, turn it so I can see the time, J's arm hair proud, conquering flags.

At Easter one spring, we're at that house you and J have in really rural LaSalle county. I wipe condensation off your keg with the hem of my dress. It runs chills over me. Water tacks through the stubble on my legs, but the whole family's outside, drinking. You've got a hooves-and-all pig swinging on a rotisserie. Drips of fatty grease fall into a steel pit. The fire hisses. Everyone's saying how much they love the sugar, the salt in the almost gelatinous air. They're going way out of their way to thank you for the whole show.

But I don't like meat, don't like parties, so I judge them all for it. I hate the entire scene. I'm disgusted. You notice. You see me pouting in the grass and you poke me in both my sides until I laugh, take off running. You chase me around your back yard. The wind gets inside the dress my parents forced me to wear and it swells up around my body. I'm embarrassed and turn to judge by the look on your face how much of me you've seen, but someone else has already wrangled your attention.

Later that afternoon, Dad's inside changing records by the song on your hi-fi and you fire bottle rockets out one of your rifles at me. Everyone's laughing, drinking still. With a family history of alcohol and yoked with what it means to work in the factories and plants in the Midwest, in factories and plants anywhere I suppose, half the family's frequently under some influence of pain and pills at our things. Everyone's quick with talk about hernia, knee, and back surgeries. But, watching you trace me with the nose of your hunting rifle, I can picture that head of the deer that hangs over your fireplace. I run away from you. I drag my fingers along the side of the house for balance. Startling pops ring. It's gunfire off the aluminum of the overhang until Mom tells you to stop torturing me. She comes out of her lawn chair like some slow, low wave, puts one hand over your eyes, the other on the muzzle, points it at the ground.

"Put that fucking thing away," she says.

You laugh, flick your lighter in her face.

Her eyes light up, playful in the yard.

She laughs as you turn the gun on her, slip another lit bottle rocket into it. She runs off. Leaving behind it a thin stream of carbon and sulfur, the firecracker screams out the barrel at her. Curling white wakes divide the sky.

Mom yelps, falls in the lawn, and the rocket shoots right past her and snaps somewhere off in the air. When she laughs her way back to her chair, I tell her that you were never torturing me. She goes cold, tells me to go get her a Coke and I do, but you're totally a charm sitting there unchecked like that: tan Carhartt jacket, black jeans, and, under a dirty Sox hat, straps of your greasy blond hair hang around like a wind sock in the rain.

J always likes to say how your hair was "so beautiful on you" that summer you two'd gotten together. I love the origin story.

You were 19, smacking nails through tar paper and asphalt shingles on the roof of your parents' house, fixing it, their old Wausau in Marseilles, Illinois. It's before your parents moved to Ottawa, passed away in that too-fluorescent retirement home that overlooks Marquette High School's football field and the Fox River that silently glides through there.

You once picked me up at your parents' place and carried me into their kitchen because I'd dumped that concrete fountain they had in their yard on myself. I know you remember, but I'm 12, trying to climb it. This big piece of it, this ten-pound angel falls on me. It pins my head to the ground for a second. Grass in my ears, I hear blades break.

You see it happen. I sit up. Blood slips down my face. It burns my eyes as you run to me, pick me up. The blood gets caught in that tight curl of arm hair you have that you say makes you look more Greek than you actually are.

"You're okay," you say, and I am.

As you hurry me into the kitchen, I cry, hang like wet bread in your arms. I can smell beer on you through all your cologne, that DV you shave with.

I take the caps off hundreds of colognes over the years trying to figure out what you wore on that day. I eventually find it at Nordstrom's. I'm walking by bright glass cabinets, accidentally swoon for you. I later buy some for a boyfriend because of you. It's an honor he never earns.

But when you carry me inside, set me up on your parents' counter, you clean blood and dirt off my face like a dad should. You hold a sponge to my eyes until I can open them again. Then, as I eat a sandwich you make me, maybe somehow picking up on something wrong between my parents and I, you go back out and reassemble the fountain quick as you can. When my parents see my face, you lie and tell them I fell in the driveway playing H.O.R.S.E. with you.

Mom still thinks I like basketball right up until the night she dies, but I barely make it back to the car that day before Mom smacks me in the mouth for the first time outside our house. Beside your parents' garage, she hits me twice.

Mom teaches me that, when fighting, the first time you get hit, it's the surprise of it, the shock of it all that gets you hit a second time even more squarely than the first. I get it once in the mouth, and then one more that digs teeth into my lips, rings my ears until I go to bed that night. She takes me by the arm, her nails lighting a fire up it, and shoves me into the backseat of the car, shuts the door.

I can tell how upset Dad is on our way back home, but also that he still is who he is and will do nothing about what Mom did to me.

Dad is Dad: lovely, mild, impractical. Even as I'm coming out of your parents' garage, I know he won't do anything, because it's him that I'm looking at when Mom leaves her passenger door open, walks right up to me, tells me that she knows you lied to her, and hits me.

I taste blood right away, but Dad stays half in, half out of the car, quietly murmurs Mom's name. What he does mostly is watch your parents' house, I assume to see if anyone's watching. I don't think anyone is, but I go to bed that night with lips tangy and brown like liver, that distant ringing going, the pain in my mouth a steady beat. And like a lot of kids do, I repeat how much I hate my parents over and over to myself in the dark of my room, but I'm just getting old enough to mean it, have cause.

It doesn't matter now to tell you this, and the thought of it may hurt you, would have probably scared you when you were alive, but your death frees me to tell you that my mind's wild that night in bed, feels hot. It's keeping me up, so I get up and go to the bathroom, turn the faucet on in the tub. When it begins to fill, I lower myself into the bath, my hands on its cool fiberglass walls, and lurch partly out of it when the heat of the water reaches my mouth. But I settle back in, wash up. Then I think about something ready in my memory, this vision. I think about you and J's origin story, you. You're on the roof on your parents' house, and I masturbate some of my anger away. Eventually, I lay in the tub with only the sound of my breathing and my body moving in the water, feeling ashamed, but buzzing. I go back to bed, pass right out after.

I love the indulgent way J tells your origin story. What she does is that she always takes a moment to say how, up on that roof on your first day together, your hair is that bleached-from-the-sun blond, filthy. She says that it blows around in what she calls "country chunks" in the wind because you don't like to get your hair wet and don't shower every day. She says that it smells like boxwood everywhere, that your shoulders are wide like the grille of a truck and that, when she comes over that first time to go out with you, she watches you for a full minute up on the roof before you notice her in the drive, wave. Her skin's tacky from the vinyl seat of the Nova she had and you sit on the ridge of the roof when you see her. You have visibly forgotten your date, but you hang the hammer on the bricks of the chimney stack. Behind her, cars buzz by on the blacktop and you smile. She forgives you right away. She says it's when she knows two things: that you will never forget her again and that she wants to marry you. It's the moment in your origin story that always reminds me how much I want to feel that way too at some point in my life.

J and I wander around the heart of Field's. Tangy perfumes settle in our mouths as we talk to one another. We're raiding the chocolate samples of this clerk whose Indian-black hair is slick in a blunt ponytail. It looks wet it's so healthy. She's beautiful, but I'm not embarrassed to admit how happy seeing a few flecks of lipstick on her teeth makes me.

J looks up.

"Look at that," she says. "The only other ceiling I've seen like that is in Paris, at a huge mall there by the Louvre. But you have to go out the back of the place to see it and the Louvre won't let you back in." She looks right at me. "It's worth it, though."

"Paris," I say.

From that atrium inside Field's, it's almost like there's pools on the ceiling, three of them surrounded by pure gold backyards. They're hovering six or seven stories above us. The neutron blue of what J says is glass looks swimmable and the gold glistens like disco. The huge ball of the chandelier is a hydrogen bomb hanging from these braided metal ropes that reach all the way up to the top and back through the ceiling we're both marveling at.

"Let's get closer," I say.

"All I know for sure is it's a Tiffany," she says, and we take an elevator up to get a good look at it.

Once there, J reads a placard to me explaining the ceiling's existence. She takes the time to start counting out loud what have to be hundreds of thousands of pieces of glass that arch away from where we stand on the balcony. I lean over, put my hand in front of my face.

The mosaic blurs between my fingers like through tears. The colors blend, become nacreous, become the prismatic springs of Yellowstone. They're county acres of waving wild flowers and I follow the spangled walls until they surround the bright, wide caverns of merchandise that make up each level. Each one glows from the lights, and the white shine of the marble floors runs off deep into the building. I count the levels all the way back to the atrium, back down to where we were.

A kid runs away from his parents there. That same pretty clerk stops him, kneels in front of him. She volleys the kid back to his family. Then they all take chocolate from her basket as she settles back onto her high heels, her ponytail spilt black ink down the valley of her spine. The mother clutches at the child's shirt. The dad starts to walk away. The family disappears into the store.

"Last time I was here, it was for Christkindlmarket, at the Daley Center," J says. She's now looking out a big, arched window onto State Street. Flags silently lash in the wind outside beyond her.

"For what?" I say, joining her. I put my hand on the metal casement around the window that ends up being too hot to touch.

"They set up a market for Christmas on Daley Plaza," she says. "It's a German thing. There's blown glass ornament tents and latkes, those potato pancakes."

"They gave us those at school once," I say.

Just a nod.

"But last time I came just to see the pigeons," she says, moving on without me. "I dragged your uncle all the way downtown to see them."

"There's something for pigeons?" I say.

"No. Veterans."

"What veterans?"

"All of them," she says. "The city put in one of those eternal flames for the veterans, like the one you saw in Washington for Kennedy, and to see the pigeons huddle up together beside it in the cold is worth the trip alone. There's dozens of them there and they all just sit there right next to the fire. You gotta see it sometime. I don't know if they'll be there this time of year, but we'll stop by it. It's right near here."

She steps away from the window, puts her hand between my shoulder blades. I can feel the sweat from my shirt when she does.

Then Brokaw.

He's leaking out this small TV over a brass and wooden bar that's as long as a speedboat, but J is inside her purse for something. She doesn't pick up on him or anything else.

"Details are coming in on Flight 232, a DC-10 bound for Chicago that crashed while trying for an emergency landing in Sioux City, Iowa," he says and continues on.

Dramatic scenes still being a surprise to see on television, everyone in the bar stops moving. Brokaw's low, stroke-like drawl hangs around. But J's oblivious, distracted. Her nose is running and she seems like the only person alive still capable of movement. She punches at her purse. Her fist bulges the bottom of it.

"I'm sorry. My allergies. I'll be right back," she says, her hand over her nose. Swinging her purse around her back, she evaporates in the garish fluorescent light that gushes from the tiled walls of a bathroom.

I don't stop her. I'm too amazed at the images that burst like solar flares on the now blaring TV the bartender's turned up.

I'm reeled into the bar.

Nobody stops me.

The plane's wing hits the ground first. The pilot manages to make it all the way to the runway, but then the wing suddenly sags and trips on the earth alongside the asphalt. The cockpit gets flattened like a swarming boxer's nose, and then it's end over end. Its fuselage is a piñata, comes apart like one. This is when pieces of the plane go up in the orange bomb of flames that consumes the video. Black bits get flung like confetti, like candy out the missing tail end of the tumbling thing and it's impossible not to fixate on the bodies those bits are.

I already know that you're on the flight. I figure that out right away but am watching the video Brokaw warned was graphic for you to somehow show. I'm who I am, so I'm certain that you're dead, because it's just flames, all of it, and it seems so fake and excessive like some cloying, corny movie that it has to either be real or too absurd to be worthy of being shown. Everyone all around me is helpless, curious. Everybody stares at the TV like a fight in a country bar.

J, suddenly there, is putting it together too, falling apart.

The space swallows her. Yet there's the true green, the endless green of her eyes. She smells like hand soap, like the floor of the woods, the sap in pine. Paper towels she'd taken from the bathroom squeeze from the bottom of her fists. She presses them to her face. Veins thicken like yarn on the tops of her hands.

I might as well not even be there. Everyone, J too, seems especially alone. I'm surprised at how nobody reaches for anyone. No one seems to notice anyone at all. We all just buoy near one another like boats in slips.

A man sitting at a table starts walking toward J. She runs at the bar, throws her arms across it, dumps a stack of glasses piled up on the end of it onto the floor. She deflates onto a stool, mewling, stares at the TV. J bleats into her hands. The man retreats. The bartender barely flinches. He gets a broom, cleans up.

I judge J for how completely tethered she is to you. I look down on her for all the times I've had difficulty approximating a J that exists without you. But something about the earnest way she's acting probably means that I'm the one who deserves to be judged.

The foundation J once showed me how to use in the bathroom by your bedroom has white lines wagging down it. Her actual skin color comes out like some streaking contrail, but Brokaw's saying that the reports they're getting confirm that there's a few survivors.

J runs out. I go after her, and in the elevator, there's a level of focus in her that gives me heart.

I think you might be alive.

I'm embarrassed by that kind of optimism now.

But, we're out the door of Field's. The still thick summer heat saps air from our lungs.

"We're running," J says, and we do.

It's maybe a half-mile to Gene and Georgetti's. J's impatient with me on our way. I try hard to keep up but know that she's angry when she slows down for me, because she's yelling at even lights and cars and beggars and workers and all things that come between you and her.

And I am one of them. I know I am.

I struggle after her, hurl myself off a high curb, stumble and stop in the middle of the road.

J's already way off.

I start up after her again.

The Daley Center, the pigeons fly right on by.

●

Dad was never going to stop Mom from doing anything to me.

At his wake, I'm mad at him for it. I treat everyone there like shit. I fight off hugs all night, and, at one point, I'm opening up the cards people've put on a table in the back of the hall. I'm looking for money for some reason. I flip the cards on the floor one by one, complain out loud when I don't find cash. Everyone's watching me. The place goes quiet. Envelopes scrape under my shoes. Mom ends up observing the sad display blankly, says nothing to anybody really. I'm upset with her for not stopping me, not doing a thing, not having the guts to hit me in front of other people, not crying. I know she won't in front of everyone, but she just sits in her chair as people wander past her. I rattle on in the back of the hall as she watches me wholly succumb to the humiliating petulance of a child several years my junior.

But I found Dad face down in the yard. Even as I'm tearing up those cards, it's a scene I can't get out of my head. Gasoline's filled the air. It's a half-cut lawn. Just out of Dad's reach, our mower rumbles. He's laying on one of his arms, caught in some queer contrapposto pile of himself. His hair blows in the wind. From even twenty feet away, it's just obvious that Dad is dead. And I'm not sure how long I stand there memorizing him like that, but it's long enough to cause real damage, long enough for a cloud of gnats to gather in orbit around me.

As soon as we get home from the wake, Mom gets herself some cereal, sits at the table.

She's in one of her places where she boxes me out. But I sit down across from her, decide to make an effort to be there for her. In this possible opportunity for us, I choose to be warm to her.

And then we don't speak. So, in that quiet, Dad's more gone. His absence is everywhere. He's not putting his coat in the closet. He's not commenting on how the house smells like whatever's in the trash, like Pinesol, like mothballs. The hollow, wooden sound of his loafers hitting the floor when he kicks them off isn't anywhere. He's not hugging me as I ignore him in my chair, holding my head in his hands so hard I can feel his wedding band press against my skull.

I close my eyes, dream of him standing there, of noise pushing at the walls, emanating from him. I dream of oscilloscopian waves.

I want to say that to Mom, but instead I'm at my most generic. I worry that, above whatever else, it's my banality that continues to give Mom yet another reason not to like me. I sit back in my chair, Mom fortified by towering walls I never felt were my responsibility to topple, already knowing that I'll be one of those abused kids who never gets to know the reasons why it ever happened.

"I miss Dad," I say instead of something better.

She looks at me, the box of cereal, pours herself some more.

"You want some of this?" she says, lets out a breath.

I get up, hug her.

With my arms just closing around her, she pops straight up and goes to grab me a bowl from the cupboard.

I see where she is, leave her to herself, the bowl in her hands.

I go to my room and come back later on. She's passed out, bottle of something, pills on the counter.

It's at Dad's funeral the next day when you and I talk about those big candles. You suggest that I keep one. They're stuck to the top of the brass holders that flank the picture the church has of Dad on the altar. The priest gives the candle to me when I ask him for it. I hold it in my lap in the car ride after.

"Set it there," Mom says, points at the kitchen table when we get home.

"Okay," I say and do.

Mom goes into the cupboards, takes out a plate, puts it under the candle. She lights it. It crackles like a 45.

"We'll light it when we miss Dad," she says, and that's exactly what we do for a while.

But I must use it too much because, one night, a couple years after both you and Dad are gone, I walk into the kitchen, find Mom staring into the dark. I light the candle, what I think is for her, sit down.

She looks up, into me.

"Don't light that all the time," she says so fast her sentences begin to come apart. "It's not for what you use it."

This symbol of Dad, a better mediator than the man, flashes between us. Mom and I look at each other for a moment like adversaries and then the moment goes.

"Okay," I say after it does.

I reach across the table, blow the candle out, go to bed, but eventually, I make sure the candle serves its nobler purpose.

J shudders when a bus wheezes by, throws up exhaust between her and the other side of the road. She slaps her hands on her jeans.

"I can't stop for you," she says, crying. "I can't."

Puzzled cars hum on the street, their drivers stunned around us in the sun. Hot asphalt rises up through my shoes. My toes stick together.

"I'm sorry," she says, hurries off.

I believe her. I believe that she's sorry. I believe that she can't stop, and as hard as it is for me, I do keep up, all the way across the Loop. I come in behind J as she blows through the front door like she intends to sack Gene and Georgetti's like Rome. The whole place is a deep, deep wooden brown and is white with shock to see us.

"A plane went down," J says to the hostess at the door.

"Okay," the hostess says, disinterested, and points at their TV.

"This is the only place he knows I'll be," she says, steps through the hostess, sits at the bar. "He'll call and I'll be here when he does."

The hostess steadies herself on her feet and rolls her eyes, her affronted expression the true imposition. She goes to the back of the house, doesn't come back. We wait at that bar for you to call for two or three hours. Various people come up to her, ask her if she needs anything. They give us pretzels. I nibble the salt off them, leave the rest in the bowl.

Behind the bar, the TV moves further and further on from your crash. It's already sports again, White Sox again, Cubs again. Red meat bleeds out the kitchen. Beer-logged rubber soaks the air and the phone rings several times, but not for J.

You never call and it's hard to see J break like a horse. She stops staring at the TV, hangs her head over the bar. Her body quiets some, but it's only after a couple hours of tears that she looks like she knows she's lost you.

A dinner rush comes and goes. We leave.

On our way home, J bucks up.

"I'm driving to Sioux City after I drop you off," she says. "I'm going to check the hospitals."

She's in and out of tears the whole way home and I wonder how many hospitals could really be in Sioux City, but we pass Bolingbrook, pass Joliet. By Morris, because I'm going home, I'm cold with worry.

Mom hasn't heard about you because we pull into the drive, our headlights slicing across the front of the house, and she's out the front door, runs toward the car.

"Where the fuck were you?" she says.

And for the first time ever, she's violent with me in front of someone other than Dad. She doesn't try to hide it, isn't afraid of J and pulls me out of the car. I smack my head on both it and the top of the door when she does.

"Where've you been?" she says again and, because I've long since learned that being silent is the only possible expedient, I say nothing.

She pushes me down in the lawn and J gets out. There's heat off the catalytic. It rattles like ball bearings in a can. There's stars in the sky. Streetlamps blot them out.

J gets between Mom and I, and I huddle into the side of the car when Mom hits J too. And this is when I learn that a good marriage makes you righteous, fearless, even as it makes you needy, because J starts to beat Mom like a mugger in the middle of the lawn. Mom looks confused, shook up, gives in. She drops to her knees like a necklace into a hand. Blood pumps out her brow. She blinks at me in the grass.

And at the moment when J could gather me into her car, take me away from Mom, has every reason to, J, instead, chooses you, the hope of you over me.

"I'm sorry," she says when I try to get to the car. She does hug me, but she volleys me back to Mom, into the yard.

Even in the moment I admire J's choice, relish the value of her singular selfishness, her understandable, fearless need to get to you. I admire that need then, and I want to feel it for someone still.

But barely a second is burned before J gets into the car and drives off after you.

The exhaust coughs out a thin blue haze. The car throws gravel onto the blacktop. Rocks tick like clocks on the asphalt. J leaves us, streetlit. The night eats us alive.

Mom, now totally gone to me, suddenly stands up, stumbles toward the house.

"Just get inside," she says.

"Okay," I say.

"Go," she says, and I do.

On our way, Mom still looks like she wants to come at me. And she does, just like she did that night, rabidly, armed and unarmed, unyieldingly, many times over the next few years. Her presence leaves my body littered with mostly hidden scars.

And you never return.

But, none of us really do.

As happens in cases like mine, I get a little bigger, a little more able to defend myself, a little more sick of Mom beating the shit out of me and I end up feeling a need to end everything between my mom and I right inside the house in which we last lived together. I don't want it to leave that place, so I make a move.

More than anything else I say here, it's this I need to tell you.

I'm graduating high school. In a red dress she loves, Mom's easy to spot in the stands in the gym. She hugs me after she finds me among the kids, and yet, still that night, with my crimson, poly gown on, I steal three bottles of pills from a friend's house. I put them on our bathroom counter at home and wait.

I'm glad that I don't see the excited look on her face when she finds the extra V, but when she takes a bunch of it a couple days later, not questioning how random pills got there, she either does or does not consider me and passes out at the kitchen table.

I find her there that night. I go into her bedroom closet, put on the same red dress she wore to my graduation, take some ground chuck out of the fridge, mix it in a bowl with that Campbell's Onion Soup Mix she knows I like, light Dad's candle, kneel under the stove, snuff out the pilot, turn the oven and all the burners on and ride my bike around the neighborhood for a while until the house blows up.

The explosion sends bits of itself onto neighboring houses up and down the block. I can hear it over two streets of rooftops, stand and watch as it brightens the sky.

I ride back through the neighborhood. I admire how beautiful it is when the smoke collects in black ponds above my house. Several stories high, firelight rolls on the clouds in the otherwise dark, these golden waves in the night. Approaching the house, ten-speed clicks give way to this raging engine of fire as it totally consumes nearly everything I know. Mercifully, soft heat flows over me like surf.

I see you while I listen to my house wheeze inside the growing fire. Maybe it isn't exactly you I see, but it's the video of you on that plane being tossed around again. I put a foot on the ground as I get to my street, still a handful of houses away, and watch a navy night brighten with flames, the approach of a half dozen emergency vehicles screaming by me.

Mine is a fire unlike yours. Not cruel, but righteous, so I stand there, the bike under me, the cool leather of the seat between my legs, and watch the ferocious thing.

Pretty soon, the roof caves in. Bits of black spin in the air. It's a sun setting on the lawn, some absolute, nuclear erasure consuming the countryside that begins to go up behind the house. Nonplussed neighbors scatter out of their homes, stunned dumb, and begin to notice me. I wait for them to come to me, the heat from the house now beginning to swallow so much air. The smoke's becoming all-consuming, acrid. The sheer volume, the high, high heat of it all makes my eyes water and I let them water, am relieved they water. I pretend it's tears when a neighbor hurries up.

"Oh," she says, frantic, desperate to do something. She leans over in front of me to look me in the eyes. She has me by my shoulders, shakes me. I drop the bike.

"Where's your mom?" she says. "Thank Christ you weren't in there. Where were you? Do you know where your mom is?"

"I don't know," I say, my eyes stung nearly shut, everything's focus soft, a cataract fuzz.

"I don't know," I say again, and my neighbor believes me.

The crowding fire thrashes against the wind as it dives into itself. The neighbor turns and takes off toward the house, runs like a child. She's shouting that Mom could still be in there.

She isn't. She's already out on the street, on a stretcher. I can hear her.

Smoke pours from the house, burns my sinuses. My nose runs.

On foot, my shoes smack the asphalt wet from the hoses. Ash settles everywhere. The street's a soaked moon.

With paramedics, cops closing in around her, Mom calls my name.

The smell of her scorched hair preceding her, Mom's covered in black soot. She's flapping her arms around, is a bug on its back, is searching for me.

I go to her.

"I was just trying to cook us dinner," she says. She finds my eyes, hers a thin, bloodshot fissure in soot, says again, "I was just trying to cook us dinner."

And everyone believes it.

She may even believe it.

I wish I could.

All of me wishes she didn't believe what she said out there, but I never learn how she made it out of the house alive, because we separate immediately after anyway. I run away and, while Mom's house is being rebuilt, I stay with J or friends the whole time, tell my friends' parents just enough of my story to ensure my shelter. Mom stays in some hotel.

But, being who she was, she never even sees the new place and I don't end up talking to her again. Instead, she keeps drinking, is fast to her pills, and after J tells me that Mom sent me tickets to my first Bulls game for my birthday, she finally kills herself with all of her problems just a few months later that year.

And when I'm in college, years later, it's a warmer day for December, the year of 9/11, the moment I stop feeling like survivors will ever emerge from anything on fire.

Still close, J and I make a special trip to see Christkindlmarket, the eternal flame at the Daley Center. On my way out the door to meet up with her, I grab those pages you gave me of Bishop's poems, take them out of my sock drawer. I put the poems, along with bread and Dinkel's Danish, into a bag, drive J and I into the Loop.

Once there, among the happy horde of people, it's onions and sugary almonds, potatoes and deep-fried doughs. Colorful ornaments hang in pop-up stand windows. Christkindlmarket is all around and every bit glorious. It's nearly all-consuming. Smoke rises from a tent where I hear that an old Polish man is blowing glass. A line of children waits to see. I'm in the shadow of Picasso's colossal sculpture, his steel gift to Chicago. Surrounded by the cold, gray granite plaza and the chatter of people talking into their glasses of spiced wine, the veterans' small flame sputters when a bus blows by.

J must be thinking of you. She's staring at the flame, leaning heavily on the railing that surrounds it, quietly crying as if she doesn't want to bother anyone with anything now. A couple dozen pigeons annularly crowd together inside the wrought iron railing.

I see you with J there, toasting me, and then, just to see how close I can get the pigeons to the fire, I toss pieces of Danish toward the flame.

"Stop that," J says. "You don't want to hurt them."

I guess I don't.

The birds, beautiful, squeeze their blood orange eyes shut. Heat passes through their feathers. Their viridescent necks quiver. They waddle toward the food, snatch it up with their beaks.

I take Bishop's pages out of my pocket, reach through the railing, hold them to the fire. The Blue Line rumbles under our feet and the words on the pages come apart, lift into the air, and fizzle out above us. They curl. J watches them. They burn and softly hiss like fuses, like hot wire to no real bomb and I tell myself I'm letting you go. I tell myself I'm letting you and Mom both go, letting it all go. Even though it's something I'll never be able to do for us, I try anyway.

And I do it for you.

But, telling you all about it, what I did to Mom, well: that's all for me.

OVER HERE[1]

My friend Maldonado killed his wife Melissa in 1995, the year after I joined the Army Reserves. I went in as a 31-Uniform, what the Army calls a Signal Support Systems Specialist. It's the guy that dies with a smoking radio strapped to his back in every war movie ever made.[2] I had just graduated from this rinky-dink high school in a very rural Indiana and had been assigned to run commo for Maldonado's unit, the 327th Military Police, this Reserve unit on O'Hare airport's property in Rosemont, Illinois. But as I emerged from a bunch of training at Leonard Wood and Fort Gordon that year, I found out that the 327th was still off on some kind of humanitarian thing in a part of the world, to be honest, I couldn't have found on a map.[3] I didn't care where they were. I was impatient for them to return. I was anxious to start my service and, when they showed back up in September of that year, I finally did.

---

[1] Or Maldonado

[2] And while he went in as a 31-U, I joined as a 92-Yankee. My job for the Army was to see to the general upkeep of a unit's office supplies. When I was in training for the job in Virginia, my platoon used to joke about how I may be the first Maldonado that couldn't hit a curveball to ever be called a Yankee. I'm not.

[3] The 327th and I were in Kuwait. We were being asked to keep Saddam Hussein at bay after the Persian Gulf War and I think we did.

I was nervous as fuck when I pulled onto the base just before six in the morning. The Air Force who manned the gate was working on my guest pass. I was sweating and a wreck, was supposed to get there early so I could fill out some paperwork, but I was late. The Air Force was taking forever to check my ID, and even with my windows down, the starch in my BDUs stunk up my car. They hung like a road sign from a hanger in the back seat. [4] I parked my car where the Air Force told me to, quickly changed, and ran onto this black asphalt plain. My new unit's matte-camouflaged Humvees ringed the lot and a few dozen soldiers were all talking to each other like very old friends.

Right away, formation came together. This lieutenant ran down a list of things he wanted us to address that weekend and relieved the unit in short order. I stood there like an idiot. I didn't know where to insert myself into any of what the lieutenant had asked us to do, was late to my first assignment, and now had no idea where I was supposed to go. I headed toward the lieutenant, had accepted that I was about to get yelled at, and knew I deserved it.

"Maldonado," the lieutenant yelled when he saw me, and someone with that name sewn into his blouse and wearing some civilian glasses ran up to us, laughed over his shoulder at a group of soldiers wandering off. "Get this guy into the office and file his paper."

The lieutenant didn't really say anything to me, but Maldonado said he would and smiled at me in such a way that I relaxed almost immediately. He showed me around for bit, introduced me to everyone, and saw to my intake

---

[4] "BDUs" are Battle Dress Uniforms – they're the camouflaged ones.

while telling me jokes. About a half hour into signing dozens of papers, he shook me to get my attention and gave me a Snickers bar he had in the pocket on his sleeve where you're supposed to keep your syrette.[5] He bought me coffee out of the machine in the office and, as we sat down on a cold metal bench beside a humming pop machine, he also started to show me pictures of his wife.

Dressed in Star Wars pajamas, Melissa was opening up a Christmas gift in just the light from the tree. She was laughing down a sidewalk at Navy Pier in Chicago, bright red lipstick on. All wrapped up, it was clearly cold out. She looked beautiful, had long red hair tied back, looked Irish.[6]

We eventually filed what needed to be filed, and then I waited for instruction from Maldonado on what I'd need to do to get through my first weekend drill, my first of what would be less than a year of drills with Maldonado before he went south, killed Melissa, and was taken away.

"You look tired," he said.

"I am," I said. "I didn't even get up this early in training. I had to drive almost sixty miles from my parents' place to get here this morning."

"Sixty miles? You know, if you ever get sick of coming, just tell them that you drive that far to get here.

---

[5] Where you're supposed to keep your morphine.

[6] She was Mexican, just like me. Her red hair was a red herring and I'll never forget how she was trying to cover her mouth with her hand in that picture. She had just started this new job at her bank. She'd been promoted to second in command of her HR department and was really nervous about it. She'd been rubbing her hands raw for a week and the cold was making it worse, but I was happy to see her smiling. She was biting one of her long fingers, and grinning right through it.

They can't make you drill, if that's the case. It's fifty, max. Seriously."

Having just met him, not sure how to respond, I sat dead still. I said nothing. It was important to me that he thought of me as the most dedicated soldier there ever was, because that's all I ever wanted to be.

"Anyway, after PT,[7] I got plans," he said and stood up, rattled keys in his pocket.

Everyone gathered in a giant, hangar-like garage for PT and flopped around doing flutter kicks. Maldonado and I never even broke a sweat. When the half-hearted PT instructor who spent her workweeks chasing down defaulted student loans via the telephone was on the other side of the garage, Maldonado showed me why he had insisted on doing his kicks in the spot we had been doing them.[8]

When we split from PT, Maldonado told the lieutenant that he had me for the weekend and the lax lieutenant didn't seem to care what we did. Maldonado and I skipped out the door where everyone smoked and around a quiet side of the building to his car.

I'll admit I was nervous to leave the base,[9] but I got into his car anyway. When I did, Maldonado already had the console open and was holding up two handfuls of quarters still in striped paper sleeves, had sunglasses on.

---

[7] Physical training.

[8] Along a brick wall, so when we rested our feet on the bricks, there'd be no sound. I was looking for fun then. I was looking for it anywhere I could. I needed the distraction.

[9] It's actually unbelievable how easy it was for that era of Reservist to sham.

Morning was wide open now and where we were parked you could smell the hash browns that puffed from the glossy red roof of the McDonald's that butted up against the far end of the 327th. The chain link, barbed wire fence that surrounded the base did little more than let the glorious smell right on through.

I'd driven by a half-dozen McDonald's on the way to the base and was starving, but because I was just a kid,[10] I had never noticed that McDonald's didn't actually open until six. I really noticed it just then.

"You're lucky I was asked to look after you," he said and tossed the quarters into the cubby under the radio, turned the car over, took off out the gate, gave the Air Force the finger out his window on our way out. "I'm going to make sure your first weekend here is easy." And the first weekend was.

We flew through an intersection with a McDonald's on the corner.

"Oh man, McDonald's," I said. I could feel my longing for it in my chest but was afraid to bring it up. Maldonado must have been able to feel how badly I wanted to go,[11] because we went through the drive-thru and he bought me my lunch. He took out this cooler he had behind his seat, pulled out some sliced pineapple, a thin sandwich of some kind and we ate in the parking lot of a largely vacated strip mall, in front of one of the few occupied storefronts: an arcade.

---

[10] A time when the real world around any base is a world that only barely exists in some modern, electric ephemera.

[11] I could.

Having grown up like a lot of kids, I suppose, playing enough video games to cause one or both eyes to often feel bulbous in their sockets, I would have never dreamed I'd spend any part of my adult life at an arcade, let alone on a drill weekend, but Maldonado got out and went into the place. I followed him, both of us still in fully camouflaged battle dress, even though I was all too aware, since I had just been informed of the rule only months before, that the government does not allow for their soldiers to be off base in their BDUs. They also don't allow for the Ranger-rolled cover Maldonado was wearing.[12] I had spent all of my training rolling my cover like his in secret. In the dim and frantic light of an arcade, I thought no one would ever notice what my hat looked like and that was the first time I realized one of the main differences between being a Reservist and an active duty member: there was this luxury of agency I had never felt during any of my training. Such agency was everywhere as a Reservist. But in that arcade, it was the first time I ever felt guilty about being so readily seduced by something, because even then, I knew it was something I hadn't yet earned.

I will say that by choosing the approach he did to welcoming me to the unit, Maldonado showed me an important part of who he was. He went so far out of his way to make me feel intimately connected to himself and the unit that it spoke to how he was as a person. He made me feel the way I did just then. I was enjoying myself, hanging out with another soldier, learning what that meant, but I was brought up to be careful not to succumb

---

[12] A "Ranger-rolled cover" is a hat where the top of it is folded in on itself so that it looks like an upended dog bowl.

to the romance of being on the run, so I was trepidatious about how I felt. I wanted to know if I had it right, in that arcade with the buzzers hissing, the echoes of youth careening from the walls. But even if I wasn't getting it right, Maldonado seemed to be. He was joyous, utterly joyous, and it was infectious.[13]

Maldonado and I played NBA Jam for quite a while, some Street Fighter, and on our way out, the noon sun up, we got back into Maldonado's car and I flipped the makeup mirror down, ran the tender pads of my fingers along the folded hem again. The crown of my head bulged the top of the cover and I felt like a real soldier for a

---

[13] I was in a terrific mood. I loved going to arcades. Melissa got me into them. When I got to hang out at one, it felt like time I got to spend with her. Her love for video games may have been second only to her love for me and we spent a lot of time playing games together when we were dating. Our first kiss was at an arcade. Racing each other on one of those motorcycle games, submerged in bells and buzzers, I lost to her and she tilted her bike over. I can still feel the wetness I wiped off my lips. I felt like I'd won life just then. Even one of our first arguments was at an arcade. I was in this shitty mood and some guy started playing a game with her while I was in the bathroom. I'm ashamed to admit that I thought she looked too happy talking to him. I was, like, eighteen at the time and got jealous. I didn't tell her why I was so pissed. I just stormed up and made this scene, but she knew. She played another five minutes with him just to make her point, and since I was still able to control myself back then, I just sulked in the corner. Turned out the guy was going to school to design video games. She was excited to discuss it with him and, once I gave her a second to talk, I was excited for her too. She was off the rails elated at the idea of going to school for that all afternoon, and would have, if it weren't for my joining the Army. She followed me all over the States for a couple years, and then I went overseas for the first time. The plan was that, once things settled down for me and she could concentrate on something other than my being on a tour, she'd go back to school. And she would have, if it weren't for me.

minute, one complete with my own critical downtime, uniform idiosyncrasies, and set routines.[14] I still love Maldonado for showing me how to get closer to it, what I know as joy, and we headed back to the 327th, both of us now Ranger-rolled.

Maybe twenty-one or twenty-two, Maldonado had spent his latest service with the 327th Reservists taking it easy, but while still active duty, he had ended up supporting a unit in Desert Storm. Every once in a while he'd tell me this and that about being over there. The stories were always brief ones that tended to trail off into laugher. Since he was a genuinely affable guy, I wrote the truncated nature of his stories off as stuff he believed too absurd to narrate, or at the very least that it was probably tough for him to talk about whatever went on over there and whatever was going on with him over here because of it.[15]

Maldonado let it go once that, during the time he was in Kuwait, in the early part of one of his tours and during those brief weeks of actual war, there were days when warbling alarms were fairly constant. He'd gotten into something where he could hear guns pop like huge

---

[14] All things you distract yourself with to keep from thinking about how your family is thousands of miles away, to keep from thinking about all the reasons you are where you are, whatever war you're in, and the fear that you either can or cannot successfully fend off.

[15] It was. It was very hard. For a while there, I was talking to Melissa about it all the time, but she didn't have any idea how to help. No one did. I regularly talked to my doctor about how I wasn't sleeping, how my moods were always off, and then I just stopped talking about myself across the board. Once it felt like I was burdening her and everyone else with something they couldn't do anything about, I thought it was a waste of time. Instead, what it was was a mistake.

paper bags nearby, could hear rockets fire and detonate close enough to feel their percussive waves pass through him. He said that you can feel gunfire and explosions in your heart, that if a wave passes through you on the off-beat, your heart flutters, but that he could not actually see any of the explosions, any bullets hissing by. He said that no one understands what it's like to be immersed in that strange level of invisible fear.[16] He would also go on to say that he shot back helplessly into what he called "some dusty nothingness," and when I asked my fellow Reservists about him in those first few drills, they told me that this was a common story in that particularly brief war, but that it wasn't really anything to get too excited about.

This was the '90s, and I'm certain that Maldonado and the rest of those active duty folks would no longer feel the same way, but it was the very early days of PTSD.[17] Nobody even talked about such a thing. The vocabulary simply didn't exist yet, at least not amongst the rank and file.

Maldonado pulled us back onto the base, the Air Force now giving us the finger as we drove back under the gate. Then he took me up to a cage, what was an actual cage where all the communications equipment for the unit

---

[16] And I'm glad they don't.

[17] It was like concussions and the NFL. We trusted our superiors and focused on our duties. And being who I was, as naive as I was, as young, PTSD was a complete mystery to me. We know now that it's been linked to the use of sarin gas over there. We know now that soldiers were breathing air that was intentionally tainted with untold amounts of pesticides, but that knowledge doesn't do anything for me now. Because back then, Melissa and I hadn't even heard of it.

was kept. He introduced me to SSG Wilson who, at least if you believed the story that he told over and over again like a rumor, had been involved in a couple major military operations over the course of his career but hadn't seen any action since Noriega. He told me that the earplugs he had been issued in Panama hung from the rearview of his car.[18] Wilson liked to make it known that he had had enough of active duty. The way he put it was that "fucking Clinton better not get in the way of [his] retirement." He played a constantly squawking scanner, said that it calmed him somehow, even though it already agitated me to no end the second I walked in the cage. We talked over it the whole time. Wilson was who I was supposed to report to and, as the drill weekends that year moved along, Maldonado handed me off to him more and more. I no longer needed as much instruction as I once did, but it was becoming impossible to miss how Maldonado wasn't the same source of joy to me that he originally was. I was starting to worry about him. He looked more tired every time I saw him, was putting on weight, and while he remained someone I looked forward to seeing, someone I considered a kind of friend, he almost seemed to be molting on a month-to-month basis.[19]

We were supposed to be getting ready for the upcoming summer drill session where I would spend the time getting qualified to fire everything I could find: the

---

[18] This is the operation where the military endlessly played G'n'R, and other shit like that, over loudspeakers in order to drive Noriega out of being holed up in the Vatican embassy in Panama on Christmas in 1989. Turns out, I think Wilson actually was there.

[19] I was suffering. Up to that point, I'd done a good job of keeping myself together, but that was changing every day.

old SAW and LAW the unit had, the M203, and the M9, M60. These are the guns that Captain America, Scarface, Bruce Willis, and Rambo shoot things up with. I ended up being pretty good at firing whatever, likely because I have always been so unimpressed with guns that I'm steady, true, thus I'm potentially lethal for someone who I now think was, even at the very peak of my service, just a glorified civilian. Those guys I trained with, those guys that got all jazzed up over just the holding of a gun, never did very good. They spent most of their training banging another empty clip on their helmet waiting for a refill from the range officer. In fact, I'd just found out that I was to spend the upcoming summer training session becoming the M60 gunner for the 327th, something that was more of an honorary title in what I knew then as the relatively peaceful Clinton era.[20]

I pulled onto the lot for a drill the weekend before we left. Maldonado was sitting on his hood, smoke streaking from his mouth and crying. When he saw me, he ducked into his car, hid his face inside.

I left him to himself, but he eventually sought me out. He found me drinking coffee in the cage with Wilson, and when Maldonado showed up, he was obviously drawn, beat.

---

[20] It really wasn't peaceful at all. Every day was starting to be a horror for me and Melissa. For months, I'd been waking up screaming. I'd started hitting her somewhere along the line. Obviously, I should be able to remember the first time I hit her, but I can't. The memory just isn't there. But the worst part is how much I do remember. I was pushing her around in public now and talking to her like she was trash and it was happening more and more.

"Get you a coffee?" I said but was fearful of how he looked. Wilson even stood up as if to keep an eye on Maldonado as he talked to me. I'd never seen Wilson try to protect anyone before, but he must have noticed Maldonado's hand on the door of the cage before I did. His knuckles were swollen and raw and slowly seeping blood. Balled up in his trembling hand was his hat.

"Sure. Let's get some coffee," he said softly, resigned, like a really old or really new prisoner.

We went to the machine and got some coffee, then went out to my car. He was so different, almost loitering, just following me around, so I took us to where he'd taken me once. I drove us to one of O'Hare's restricted areas, to this access road that runs along the end of one of the colossal runways. Being parked at the end of a runway that only a small number of people had access to should have been more thrilling than it was.[21] Every few minutes, as Maldonado and I started talking on the hood of my car, planes would drop out of the sky over us, swing down and squeal when they hit the runway. Maldonado had brought me there before, and because he said that it might be fun, it had been fun. Even that first plane that went over us out there again was amazing: the plane's huge wheels down, looking like they'd crush my car. The jet wash dropped a blurry veneer onto us, smeared the blue of the sky. But as they kept coming down every three or four minutes, by the third one, I wanted them to stop. I wanted to ask about why he looked as rough as he did, but instead, he wanted to talk for quite a while about a number of things that he

---

[21] What it was was terrifying. It was terror that was on my face. I had come out there to admit what I'd done to Melissa, because I had to tell someone.

said never seemed to be of any interest to anyone: what he'd been doing since he'd gotten back from Kuwait, whether or not he liked his actual job, sports, celebrities, his hobbies, and whatnot.[22]

I did eventually ask him about his hands, and when I did, he put them in his pockets, started in on a story about when he and his wife went to Mexico for their honeymoon.

Maldonado and Melissa got married before he shipped out for Desert Storm, but he said they put off the honeymoon until recently. They were just on it. In that time between the unit returning and my reporting, they had slipped in a quick week of honeymooning. They stayed in a hostel called the Hacienda Mariposa in downtown Playa del Carmen, where skinny cats and dogs still roam but get run off by the local police into the pitted, cracked streets that stretch away from the main area of the downtown.[23]

---

[22] I don't think it matters now, but I loaded and emptied trucks for UPS. I've got the shoulders to prove it, and even though I loved my time in Chicago, I was an Eagles fan. I also loved the Sixers, the Phils, and Mia Sara, but mostly because she looked like a brunette version of Melissa. You know, no one but Melissa knew this, but I had a guitar in my closet and was trying to learn to play.

[23] The dogs and cats get run off by the local police because people complain about how many of them are so skinny you can see their ribs as they walk up to you and beg for help. It's hard to see. Melissa and I took off out of the hotel one night, brought some bread with us to give to the strays. We found a few in an alley and gave them some of what we had. Melissa started crying and we just set everything we'd brought on the ground, went back to the hotel. Being unable to sleep was common enough at that point, but I sat up in bed thinking about those strays for a while. They were just all on their own. I silently cried in the

Downtown Playa is only a few blocks long, and after nights stuffed with flashing bar lights that never really go out, those few blocks are filled with shops that spill out onto the sidewalks in the mornings for the tourists to pick up things, take pictures of them holding things they seldom buy.

Maldonado and Melissa had done the same down there, taken pictures wearing hats that look like frogs, that look like fruit, like monkeys. They had eaten the freshest mangos, the freshest muskmelon they'd ever seen. They'd bought real vanilla extract, sent it back to America via the post, spent their mornings on a beach in front of a restaurant where they drank tangy citrus drinks out of glasses slick with condensation. They watched boats shoot out a hundred feet from shore to retrieve from a fisherman there someone's wiggling kingfish or bonefish, bring it back to shore, slaughter it on a small, bloody table beside the restaurant, serve it shortly thereafter to tourists just like them. Maldonado said that the sand was the color of blood orange pulp around that little table, but it dried in moments in the strength of the sun.[24]

---

dark. It was impossible not to think of them just trying to survive and probably failing.

[24] I was thinking about terrible things sitting there. I thought the whole scene was disgusting and that it said disgusting things about us. I was already pretty unrecognizable to myself, but I got a moment of true peace sitting at that table with Melissa. Her voice drew me in. I leaned across the table into her. The sun was so hot on my back that I almost didn't kiss her. I almost sat back in my chair, like a fool, but I went for it. She smelled like the rose perfume she liked, like lotion and roses, and feeling the vein on her neck pulse through my lips made my toes curl in my sandals.

Maldonado and Melissa tried to recreate the experience of the great coffee they drank during the neon-singed nights they'd shared in Mexico, the conversations they'd had in those quiet mornings, during those first few days back in America, but in between planes Maldonado told me how he and Melissa had also gone diving down in Mexico. They had swam in the warm water of a cenote behind a colorful house Jerry Garcia used to own when he was alive, had dived deep into an underwater cavern.[25] The instructor took their hands, pulled them under the surface of the dark water and pointed out the wavering headlamp light of a film crew who he said had been retrieving whole skeletons, old wooden instruments, and cups and bowls from the bowels of the earth.

But Maldonado told me that, on their last night there, he and Melissa went out to a bar with the instructor, had all danced to music on way too loud, had all drank so much that Maldonado's mind had gone south on him.

"I came back from getting drinks to see the instructor talking to Melissa," he said, my car running and humming under us. "I just thought that he was sitting way too close to her, so we got to yelling at each other and I hit him so hard that you could see the bottom row of his teeth through this two-inch-long fissure I gave him in his lower lip."

He laughed for a second, but through it, I could still see how much this really hurt Maldonado to say. There

---

[25] Melissa wore her favorite swimsuit that day. It had pineapples printed on it. She loved pineapples exactly that much. I ate them all the time, just to think about her.

was no macho pride.[26] He was embarrassed, sweating, and the laugh was awkward.

"I was nervous about the Mexican police the rest of the trip, right up until we flew back over Havana. Melissa waved at Cuba as we passed over it, said *hola* as if the entire country could hear it."

As he spoke, his face changed from wildly animated and out of control to something much more placid, then to some kind of death mask, but still he talked about love.

"I loved that moment with her, you know. She was so cute. I'd give anything to remember her face then, but I can't see it now. Anyway, I leaned over her to see what she was looking at and Cuba was so washed out from the air. You could see buildings even, but it was like the whole country was left in the sun too long. Melissa ran her hand up and down my back and the airplane sounded like that snow on TV when the show goes off."

He was opening up out there, and I'm not sure why he was doing so to me, but the air electric, I knew he was revving up to tell me something he had done that he was deeply ashamed of.

He leaned into me. The hood clanged as he put his fist in my face, showed me how the knuckle on the hand he hit the instructor with still slipped in and out of its socket. He kept it up. He slipped his knuckle in and out, in and out. He did this more than enough times to unnerve me and he looked so fucked up. His skin clutched for his eyes.

"I think she's been afraid of me lately," he said. "And I think I've given her every reason to be."

---

[26] No pride at all.

I said nothing, just stared at the scab that had opened up on his hand. Blood ran in between his knuckles now, and I didn't want to know why his hands looked the way they did anymore.

He started to tell me anyway.[27]

"I went to bed last night, like normal, and I just woke up hitting her," he said, put his hands back down. He waited for a plane to pass over. It slid by so slowly. Then, he twitched and cried.

"I don't really know what happened," he said. "All I can think about is that, maybe if she had made more noise, I would have woken up."

I thought about what noise it would have had to have been to wake him, but Maldonado went on to say that, what woke him up eventually was the pain in his hands, not anything else, and then he said that he had left Melissa there, at home. She was still lying in their bed.

He didn't have to actually admit to me that he had killed Melissa in his sleep, that he had beaten her to death.[28] I tried to think Maldonado was saying anything but what he actually was, but I sat out there avoiding his eyes because of how I was suddenly a little afraid of him. Part of me feels bad about that now, but I didn't know

---

[27] And it was the hardest thing I ever had to do. My plan was to tell you how much I loved Melissa, too, mixed in with everything else. But I couldn't really say out loud what I did to her and it doesn't matter now. The starting to tell you was impossible enough.

[28] And I don't think I could have, because I never really had to say it out loud. I pleaded out in court and thought myself a coward the whole time. The PTSD the prison shrinks offer up as a potential lifeline to me now feels like a reason, I guess, all these years later, but it's not any kind of solace. It's nothing like it.

what I was dealing with and I don't think it would have helped to know.

Traffic was backing up on the street that led to the base. It filled up with the local police. They were queued in a long line in front of the gate, ten to twelve cars deep already. The Air Force was out of their booth and was talking to the cops through the window of one of the cruisers. When still more cops came, Maldonado noticed, and he suggested that we go back. So we got into the car and headed toward flickering blue and red.

One thing I remember thinking was that, considering what he had done, the MPs of the unit, most of which were troopers for the state and the county for their real jobs, and likely confused and outraged but trying to adhere to some duty, they treated Maldonado and the local police with an admirable amount of restraint. They were eventually asked and subsequently agreed to detain him and bring him to the gate. A number of us quietly walked Maldonado off the base, out past the Air Force. They looked solemn now and we handed Maldonado unceremoniously over to the local police. Having been to his house, having been the ones to have found Melissa and seen the visceral aftermath of what he had done, the locals banged him around when they cuffed him, shoved him into a cruiser. They were cold, but as disciplined as you could hope. Maldonado never looked back at me. He never looked back at any of us. The police cars all broke apart and he was driven away.

We still finished our drill that weekend, because Reservists, due to something that always felt like some overly strict adherence to a futile rule, never cancel a drill weekend. But nobody said anything to one another after some initial back-and-forth about what had happened. We all went our own ways. Melissa's death did not bring any of us together to talk about it like I thought it might. All around me I could feel the other Reservists focusing on prep for the summer drill session.

The whole thing seemed easier for them to accept than it was for me, and because I never ended up going active duty, I don't think I'll ever really know why that is. I do know that it was never more clear to me how far apart we were, or at least how far apart from them, and from Maldonado, I felt.[29]

I went back to my cage to find Wilson. When he saw me coming, he didn't say anything, but he looked as though he'd been standing ever since I'd left with Maldonado. When I came in and sat down, he did too. He even put an arm around my shoulder for a second until he got up to turn on the scanner. We sat there together for about half an hour listening to the sounds scatter along the concrete floor. Then, in what was maybe only ten seconds of dead air, he started in again on his story about Panama. This time, like I'd never heard a word of it, I listened to every detail he offered. I asked him questions about it, asked him what he did when he came home, what that was like, and then I asked him whether or not he liked his actual job, sports, his hobbies, and he told me. He must have talked about all that for a good, solid hour or two.

---

[29] Preserving that distance is one of the most important things soldiers do. I don't think that either my story or yours should be considered the universal soldier experience, but all I know is that Melissa and I paid the highest possible price to preserve that distance you felt, so I couldn't be happier to have done at least that part of my service well.

I stopped showing up to drills shortly thereafter. I told the 327th, when this new, less lenient lieutenant finally called months later, what Maldonado said to. I told the Army that I had moved back to my parents' house, that I was now living outside a fifty-mile radius from a base. I didn't actually move back to Indiana, but I told them I did. The Army never knew any better. For six years after that, I ended up on the IRR, this list that you go on where you don't drill, but the Army can call you back up, and when 9/11 hit, I watched the second plane disappear into the side of the World Trade Center, both buildings fall, while I feared the phone.

The Army never called.

You know, I still can't see a McDonald's, still can't see a plane land without picturing Melissa, alone in her bed, Maldonado on the hood of my car. Sometimes I wonder if Melissa had opened her eyes as Maldonado came down on her with the weight of a landing plane. What I still can't figure out is, even though I believed him when he said he was asleep, I wonder if Maldonado's eyes were open when he did what he did. I can't quite decide if it would make any difference, but I'd like to think that Melissa's eyes were closed right up until the end, that both their eyes were.

I'd like to, if only to spare her heart, if only to spare both their hearts.[30]

---

[30] I'd like to, too, but when I finally did open my eyes, hers were looking right at me. They still are.

NOT ORIGINALLY FROM NEW YORK OR: THE MISUNDERSTANDINGS

Okay look, I'm willing to admit to you that I'm not originally from New York (I'm aware of what that says to you all about me), but when I got off the train and started asking people if anybody had heard of a bar called Mitzvah, because a guy that used to be my alive friend told me that he was going to meet me there in celebration of my recent move to Manhattan, I nevertheless feel okay telling you that I got more than my fair share of shitty looks on 77th and Lexington (or Lex to the newly, enthusiastically initiated, like me).

I was there alone, on the corner, a warm and noisy wind pushing up from the 4/5/6 train grate I was walking over blowing softly up my pant leg, thinking about how it must be considerably harder for some people to avoid smelling like urine than I would have originally thought and how if you find yourself frequently falling asleep on public transportation, then I have to tell you that your life has likely gone completely off the rails.

I suddenly stopped and felt ridiculous (or not at all like some masculine version of Marilyn Monroe) and was shaking my head, because I had just gotten my then still-alive friend's admittedly pretty decent pun (however, his heart attack – brought on by thick, cholesterol-lined arterial walls—and, also, the fight that brought it on, had not yet happened).

I had already spent the whole time on the train on the way there trying to look up where this Mitzvah might be located on my smartphone that had no signal, which didn't occur to me to be a problem since I'm originally from a small town in Illinois (a fact about my past from which you should not draw any neat or major conclusions as I do not feel I am somehow wholly representative of someone from there). This small town I'm speaking of (LaSalle) is located about an hour and a half outside a recently even more violent Chicago (sadly, groups of teenagers are beating the hell out of random folks on the Magnificent Mile there now, and in the middle of the day no less, but I don't relay these kinds of things to New Yorkers. Chicago doesn't need that). Chicago is a place where the trains run above the ground in what I would say is a more uncivilized manner (think north of 125th Street in Manhattan and the outer boroughs). These neighborhoods by and large seem over-determined to be "vibrant" – a word I repeat here since it seems to be some euphemism used by fuckface real estate guys to describe neighborhoods these same assholes were saying I should avoid upon my moving to NYC and that are chronically, albeit reluctantly I'm sure, embracing their largely economically bummed-out (depressed) status. Like the El in Chicago, these elevated rails seem to hover over these neighborhoods in New York that hang from the tracks there like gaunt torsos, decaying and pulling from their iron ribs and steel spines. (Let's face it, maybe those fuckface real estate guys were right. How the hell should I know?)

But standing there in the late evening, I was doing so like some kind of weird, tall toddler and naively unaware of why I'd been hung out to dry in this manner by my friend intentionally. I was afraid to take my phone out (although I eventually would anyway) because my parents, when I called to wish my mom a happy Mother's Day, had just warned me that everyone is stealing iPhones at every opportunity in New York. She said, "They're pushing people onto the tracks out there," and I found myself starting to buy into this paranoia (which seems to have something to do with the vulnerability of being totally unaware of your surroundings and being made of the kind of stuff that makes you believe everyone, absolutely everyone, is capable of terrible things and also having been born with the innate ability to imagine a lot of terror and blood into any tableau – yes, even that of the Upper East Side).

All of this, I should point out, was likely exactly what Marty (my then still-alive friend) had anticipated I would be feeling and was almost certainly going to make me tell him all about once I found where he actually was.

Marty was probably watching me from some window or one of the vaguely Europeanesque patios that always have wonderful dogs tethered to them (I myself have a fawn-colored Chihuahua named Terrance that actually looks quite a bit like a fawn). Marty was almost certainly chuckling at me and how I was there swearing to myself, obviously angry with him and anxious to tell him that I didn't appreciate being led astray.

But when he came out of a door smiling at me, I'll admit that I dropped all of this, all the pretense, and it wasn't long before I was happily corralled into his honest and convivial laughter as well as suddenly more relaxed and aware of that stench that I've come to love since I'd finally gotten my shit together (well, married someone whose shit was already significantly better together than mine was) and actually made the move to New York instead of just visiting it. Now, telling you this story of how my friend Marty died from some distant place in the future, I feel confident in saying that what I think that smell that soaks the New York air actually is, is some mixture of century-old bakeries, not quite as old refuse (organic, human based – and inorganic, human by-product), and the gloriously familiar Starbucks, the sweet-smelling, rolling-skyward smoke of roasted nuts and, perhaps, maybe even some kind of kebab (most definitely some kind of kebab).

Anyway, my friend Marty, who strode out of the front of a bar, put his arms around me, and forced a hug upon me, did indeed die later on that night (all of which I'll get to describing, but take note that it will not be dramatic and has nothing to do with what people who have no idea what it's like to live in New York think happens to people who have some idea what it's like to live in New York; i.e., the actual scene says nothing about NYC itself. Instead, it says a lot about Marty's hardened arteries, which were an import from the Midwest, and him having, at least once for me to witness when we were roommates there, a pound of bacon for dinner). His death was surprisingly simple, direct, fast, like New York itself. It will not break your heart. It did not mine.

After retrieving me from the street, Marty led me into some random bar. Just inside the door stood two rather large guys who looked as if they were strong, stacked white pillars of marble that had to have been erected there by a team of engineers. These two "rather large" guys were having to be told by the bartender to put the dartboard back on the wall that the bigger of the two was holding gleefully (dimly) in his hands.

I should say here that I glared at them. I glared at them the way I glare at people I don't approve of, and when they saw me doing so, I had to try very hard to not look away immediately. But, instead, they did and I chalked that up as my first major victory toward acquiring the same aggressively entitled attitude that I recognize in my now fellow New Yorkers, an attitude demonstrated at crosswalks all over town where there is always someone who must stand farther into the street, who must cross the street ahead of me (I can't be the only person who's just praying to see one of these super-eager folks dragged half a city block by a Yellow Cab, can I?). I thought that this was all part of my maturation as a New Yorker, that you must never look away and that all space everywhere is inalienably yours but, as it turned out, I may have had it all wrong.

The two "rather large" guys went back to whatever ridiculous madness they had been up to before I arrived and Marty led me to a table in the middle of the bar ringed with three strangers. We sat down next to these strangers and, that smell bars always have, dry rubber soaked in beer, in all honesty made me, if only just for a fleeting moment, think of growing up back home, a saccharine, sentimental something I quickly stifled.

"What happened was," Marty said about me, "was – well, you should have seen him. You should have seen him.

I should've taken his phone, the fucking paranoid, I should've taken it just to prove a point."

Other than Marty, as I said, I was surrounded by strangers. I didn't end up liking any of them, so feel free to picture them however you will, as they possessed no discernible or desirable traits to speak of. They just looked like canned people, placed onto bar stools like from some terrible sitcom kit (all of them men, unfortunately – women I seem to repel as if I chronically smell of the Eastern European sausage I love so much). Rest assured there were goatees, clever t-shirts, and all sorts of lame shit like that (I really was expecting more tailored clothing on the men of NYC. You disappointed me, New York). Thankfully, they were not around for long. However, while they were there, they liked to say "uh-huh."

"Uh-huh," I said.

I said this because I was laughing along with them (mocking them) as they seemed to be thoroughly enjoying making fun of my greenness, my cherry behavior and how it was being lavishly recounted for their enjoyment (I use the word "cherry" here because of having been briefly in the military – no action – the Clinton years, thank you). I played along in order for us to move on, which we soon did.

"You should have moved here like ten years ago," Marty said later. "You're late. I may have been late."

"Why? Because you moved here ten years ago?" I said.

This was not the first time I've heard this sentiment about New York. There is seemingly no shortage of people telling other people that New York was amazing in this time, in that time, almost any time other than the present day. I was (and am) frankly sick of hearing about it.

"No," Marty said. "People told me when I moved here back then that New York was dead and I guess I have to say that I'm starting to believe them."

(Dead? Like art? Paul McCartney? Going to the movies? The collective sex-life? America? – ho-hum).

Marty had apparently also heard these same sentiments but seemed willing to resign himself to the idea. I wasn't (and am not).

"What?" I said.

"Yeah," he said. "Maybe."

The others leaned in.

"You know, I guess the cabs still won't go north of 110th," I said, trying to fit in and seize the attention I had stumbled upon, but really what I was actually doing was just appropriating something a cab driver had told me and which was one of the few pieces of commentary I felt I could offer on the subject of the city at all.

I believed that I was being ballsy, brash, and political by saying this, which I wrongly believed all people in New York were, but the others had leaned out mid-sentence and were waving at someone deep into the smokeless bar (No smoking? Maybe New York was over. Where have all the poor decisions gone?). Then they got up and left the bar (I never saw them at Marty's funeral or again). However, their welcome departure at the time left Marty and myself talking to each other across a sticky high top, drinking (heavily).

"The cabs still don't like to go above 110th street," I said, thinking that maybe it was the phrasing or, perhaps, something in the grammar of the sentence that had prompted the lack of response and, for whatever reason, I was determined to elicit one (I guess I wish now that I could have picked up on the scene that Marty's instincts were trying to avoid).

"It used to be 96th," he said. "What's the new place like?"

I turned around as I answered him (the answer was the faithful cliché that everyone is comfortable with – small, the apartment was small – so many of them truly are. This notion that all New York apartments are small is not something that I can complicate. Also, I cannot tell you how to avoid paying the two grand in painful broker's fees it takes to rent an apartment here. Okay, broker's fees. Think about how when you used to rent a movie on a whim, say Boogie Nights, at Blockbuster and lost it and they charged you 75 dollars to replace it. Remember how angry all that made you? Now, imagine that fee is 2,000 dollars. That's a pain that never goes away. So much so that once you manage to move to New York and gag up that drug-mule-sized broker's fee, you cling to that little apartment like life.).

The waitress came by too often with more drinks.

We drank.

"Fuckin' Cubs fans and shit," I said later.

We were drinking really quite a bit.

"Fucking Cubs," he said.

On this we agreed wholeheartedly and it was a conversation that we were surprisingly able to track fairly well and without much effort. The Cubs were and are indeed shit. Maybe it was the familiarity of such a conversation, the triteness of it all, that put me at ease. Maybe too at ease.

I was drunk, and although this is not to excuse the following statement (as I don't believe that it needs to be excused – I might be willing to go as far as saying that it needs to be explained, maybe), everyone looked to me visually as though they'd lost their edge, while all the things we were suddenly willing to say to each other out loud hadn't. We were talking about this and that, but somehow settled on a class about world music that Marty and I had taken in school together at Northern University in DeKalb, Illinois.

"There's nothing inherently interesting about Africa," I eventually said midway through the conversation.

"Who?" Marty said.

"Africa – it's not inherently interesting," I said.

"What's that?" someone said.

For whatever reason, Marty was now only loosely listening (I didn't know it, but someone else was apparently listening really closely).

"Africa," he said. "Yeah. Okay."

"What?" I said.

"Did you know," he said, "I went to Times Square for this business lunch–"

Marty was obviously trying to change the subject and I knew it. I could feel him trying to urge the conversation elsewhere, to less risky places, and it pissed me off. But, I let him anyway (I shouldn't have. I should have at least finished my thought. This likely would have saved him).

"Where?" I said, indulging him instead.

"Havana Central. I like the steak fries," he said. "Did you know that nobody out here knows what I'm talking about when I say 'steak fries?'"

"Really? What about 'dish-to-pass?'" I said.

"Hey!" someone said.

"Yeah, and 'dish-to-pass,'" Marty said, nodding. "But, nobody anywhere outside of Illinois Valley knows what that means."

(It's another term for what you bring to a potluck – Christ, hopefully "potluck" is universal. I'm telling you this flat just so we can move on to these odd interjections that I'm sure you'd rather I focus on).

"Anyway," he continued, "I was in Times Square and we left together and these guys were from Nashville–"

"Oo! What's that Bar-B-Q place there?" I said.

"I don't know," he said.

"Jack's," I said. "It's Jack's."

"It's good?" he said.

"It's tremendous."

"Anyway," he said, "they insisted that we all had to get two pops each at one of the carts down there. I guess they thought that they were making some kind of point."

(http://en.wikipedia.org/wiki/New_York_City_soft _drink_size_limit).

"Hey. What did you say earlier about Africa?" someone said.

What happened then was that I turned around. I turned around and I shouldn't have. I should've just continued to ignore what turned out to be one of the "rather large" guys (clearly pissed – angry and drunk) and his friend (also, clearly pissed – same). They were, instead of fairly harmlessly holding a dartboard on the far side of the bar, now looming huge behind me.

"Nothing," I said.

"No, hey," the smaller of the two "rather large" guys, who would eventually hit me with something and leave me bleeding out my mouth in the gutter and flee deep into one of those uniquely New York nighttimes after Marty tried to hit one back but instead crumpled awkwardly to the ground holding his chest, said to me, "it's not okay what you said."

"Why don't you go back to whatever it is that you two fucks were doing?" I said turning back around.

Okay. I was bold that night. I was smiling into my glass of beer I was so bold. But, as it turned out for Marty, I was too bold.

I'm not sure what it was exactly that I went on to say to these two guys that escalated the situation to a level that they could no longer ignore. It could have been anything but, just saying, Marty was no help. He just let me keep talking. This could also be because, as it has been explained to me later, what happened to us that night does not usually happen in New York. Usually, I was told, in New York these sorts of confrontations don't occur for a variety of reasons that I (again, having just moved there that morning) wouldn't have had the opportunity to find out yet. The reason this altercation happening to me was seen as lacking verisimilitude has since been described to me in this way: One of the reasons New York works is these sorts of things just don't happen that often; that the magic of the city is that most everyone minds their own business, otherwise these sorts of things would always be happening was what I was told (this is something I don't believe). I'm not even going to pretend that I have any idea why these types of things don't happen more often. I don't think it's something you can know. However, I have always had a tendency to be someone whom strangers have felt an overwhelming obligation to rein in; yes, even in the face of the NYPD (I'm still not used to the camouflaged men and women with AR-15s loitering in Grand Central Station) and, what would be, the almost unavoidable assault and battery charges. Fact is, all this did happen and, somewhere in the middle of all the things that I was saying to them, I had gone too far for these two to look the other way or, as it was later put to me, what would happen to me in the Midwest, like some kind of anomaly, ultimately did happen to me in the apparently/supposedly/fantastically fight-free New York.

It was right around that time that I failed to foresee that I was going to end up in the hospital with my friend dead because of his trying to protect me and what I felt was my right to talk with Marty about the difference between being a racist and prejudiced or even just my being an egocentric asshole (which was why I brought up Africa in the first place). I'd be willing to have a conversation about how I may have been wrong for doing it in a bar, but I didn't think about the trickiness of the subject at the time because when I said what I said, I did have a cursory look around the bar and saw no black people (my one admittedly really racist error that turned out to be fatal for Marty). So, I thought that I'd be fine, but in hindsight I clearly wasn't and I'll admit that I was probably operating then on what may be a profound misunderstanding of what can be said and what cannot be said, as well as what is likely my misunderstanding of the issue of race itself.

This was my mistake.

Now, to the point that I'm sure everyone wants to see for some reason that I wish I didn't understand (as I too love action movies).

The smaller of the two "rather large" guys (the way I described them to the kind of unsympathetic police later) grabbed me by the back of my shirt and yanked me off the stool. I spilled my beer on the bartender who was reaching for something I never got to see because of my being dragged outside (I'm small – 5'7"ish, light – 160ish). I could hear Marty arguing–well, pleading my case. He was saying that I wasn't really a racist, that all I was about to try to highlight was the difference between the word racist and the word prejudiced, but that I have a tendency to try to make these kind of distinctions in conversations in a historically inflammatory and slightly inappropriately off-color manner and that I was harmless and really pretty supportive of all things that Marty thought these guys would think I should be in support of. He went on to say that he was sorry that I wasn't lucky enough to emerge from the womb fully-formed (something I had said to him once before), that he was sure I meant something by the use of the word "inherently" (I did) and furthermore, that he was certain that I could explain myself properly if given the chance (which I didn't get and doesn't matter now). All the while, the guys he was trying to convince of this were saying "uh-huh," but they didn't mean it.

Once I had been lugged outside, I was allowed to stand up on my own feet before I was knocked down again by being punched right around the ear area (I had turned my head to avoid being hit in my face – which exposed my inexperience in fighting, since being hit there almost always results in lightheadedness, I was told later, if you're not knocked out completely by the blow). I staggered and Marty (still okay), who I'm sure had been hoping it wouldn't come to what it had come to and was likely relatively confident of the likelihood of his receiving quite a beating should he choose to defend me, courageously defended me anyway.

This was his fatal mistake.

My "rather large" guy hit me one more time in the mouth with something (I'm not sure what) and I fell immediately to the ground. I was aware enough of my surroundings, in addition to being hyper-aware of the current violent situation, to not at all like how I was now literally lying in the gray slurry of filth in the gutter that my mother thinks streaks everywhere all across New York, and actually kind of does.

But just before I passed out from the blow, I lay there wishing that I had fallen the other direction because the way I fell, I was unable to avoid seeing Marty's last moments as the two "rather large" men turned on him together and put him down with a load of viciousness I would rather not describe; in fact, I actually refuse to. And then this was when he (my old friend Marty), after crumpling awkwardly to the ground holding his chest, died.

THE NOISE OF
YOUTH

It's '85, summer, Ottawa, Illinois. We're deep into the cicada rutting season. They're everywhere. They hiss in all the trees. I'm nine and I'm dropped off at you and your grandma's. My parents are sitting in the drive. Mom waves. The orange sleeve of her blouse flags around her arm. Dad's talking to her. She turns to him, back at me. They wait until your grandma opens the door and then they take off down Route 6, go to work. I follow your grandma in. I'm not there two minutes before I already miss the dog I couldn't bring over, and from the window by the door, I watch my parents' Pontiac drive off. It's a pale blue toy and vanishes into a small cluster of low buildings on the edge of town. Your grandma doesn't really say much to me, never really does. She's shitty like that and wanders off into the living room, where she always sits in her recliner for hours, ignores everyone, lets anybody do anything to anyone.

The Cubs are on again. Steve Stone's voice slips through the air like someone tuning something. Harry Caray garbles out play-by-play in your hot house. The heat feels like it has mass, a lot of it. It's always that way. I'm sweating already and the living room smells dry. Your whole house smells strange, like old magazines. It's got to be the wallpaper. It curls at the seams, casts slivers of shadows on the walls, is brittle, flakes onto the floor when I run my hands over it. Your radio's on upstairs and your grandma finally says something, tells me to stop standing in the living room, to run on up and see you.

I do.

I knock on your door and you open it like a magician. You hover your hand over the bed all dramatic and slow. On top of the comforter is a stack of mags, this Playboy. There's some tapes I don't know. The comics you told me I could borrow are there. Patchouli burns in a colorful wooden dish.

I stare at the Playboy.

You hand me the comics, put everything else into a backpack.

I flip through The X-Men, The Uncanny, through Wolverine.

"I've read these," I say, try to hand them back to you.

You nod at the stack.

I shuffle through it.

At the bottom of the pile, it's a Punisher in a plastic jacket. I know it's for me. You don't have to say anything.

You step to me, hook an arm around the back of my neck, tug me into you. It comes to me that this could be your version of an apology for something that happened the last time I'd come over. I don't blame you for this, but you'd thrown that pop can at a tree and it had opened up, flown back at us, hit me in the chest. It had knocked me down, made it hard for me to breathe for a while. We laughed about it later, but you had been visibly concerned. It ended up leaving that baseball-sized black hole of a bruise I hid from my folks. I had to sleep on my back.

You ask to see it.

I lift my shirt.

"Gruesome," you say. "Awesome."

I smile.

You smile back.

You turn up your tunes on a ghetto blaster that sits on top of your bureau. You ask if I like the song that's on, wag a cassette case of Corey Hart in front of me until I take it.

"Is this this?" I say, tap on the case.

You grab at your crotch, a huge smile on your face, don't answer me.

"Cock too big for the underwear," you say. "Got to go empty the thing out."

You do, and with the sound of you taking a leak jingling down the hall, I wait in your room, read the names of the Corey Hart songs, study the cover. I want his Wayfarers, his motorcycle jacket, the v-neck Hart has on. I want the earring in his ear. I want his haircut, start planning how it will all go over at school. I repeat the name Corey Hart over and over again. I want to remember it, get Mom to buy the tape for me at K-Mart.

You flush, and from the hallway, you ask if I want a Coke. I do and you thump down the stairs.

The sunlight through the lattice of your window is a bright, but a sick, golden brown. I can make out the edges of it while it's still in the air. The beams look sharp and boxy, like the glass chimes that hang outside Mrs. Streator's classroom. I often stare at those chimes, try to anticipate when the wind will make them scrape the corrugated siding of the school, tick hash marks on my desk when it happens.

Your room is even hotter than it is downstairs. I chop at the sunlight. The air curls. Dust floats around in the dull amber light like gnats out over a pond.

You come back.

We leave.

We're outside and head out across that adjacent graveyard. We skid up a huge hill still slick with the morning. Our shoes squeak on the damp grass and we cut through the edge of those woods that surround your place. It smells like rich potting soil inside, in the shade. That clearing with the foundation we'd been telling each other the backstory of is there. It's an ancient Indian burial ground, I say, because I can't come up with anything better, had just gone on vacation with my folks, watched Poltergeist at this iffy Best Western outside Cheyenne, Wyoming. You say that it's where they put the dead radium girls when they closed the factory downtown in the 1930s.

"Do you know they're buried here?" you say and dig at the dirt with the toe of your shoe. "I bet there's bones."

But I know that the gray foundation isn't big enough to actually be what you say it is. The story my parents made me watch about those girls had just been on TV. I saw it. It said that there were dozens of girls who got cancer and died because they liked their teeth to glow in the dark. It talked about how they used radium-laced paint as a rouge. When a commercial had come on, I had to ask Mom what rouge even was. She put her fingers to her cheeks, rubbed them, then went to the cabinet, showed me, put some on all three of us. Dad pinched his mouth up, shimmied on the couch like a marionette. We watched the rest of the show. I went to bed looking like a doll, woke up with makeup on my pillow, the clay smell of it in my nose.

There's a depression inside that foundation of broken concrete that juts from the ground. It just sits there like an open mouth. We lay down inside it to see if we can fit. We can. We're there for a few minutes, watch the limbs of trees rock above us, talk about KISS. I say it's a band that I heard about from Chad Stills. He's that fat, sweaty, quiet eighth-grader I know you know who sits in the back of the bus, listens to music all the way to school. I tell you that he doesn't seem to care about anyone, even ignores my staring at him, but I want you to think that KISS is good. You do, but you already know who they are. You say Stills was in fifth grade when you left for high school, that he wasn't fat last you saw him, that he was just a kid, that he wouldn't remember you. You say things like that all the time, seem to believe you're particularly forgettable.

You're not.

Chad Stills requires some endurance. I let him slip the warm foam of his Walkman earphones over my head because I'm afraid of Justin Bell. Justin's a stringy, fair-skinned neighbor of mine. You don't know him, but you know his older brother. Some nights, it's his older brother who beats Justin to the point where he ends up missing school. The thing is that Justin has a habit of taking this out on me. We'll both be in our driveways waiting for the bus and he'll fight to get on first, sit up front. And every time he survives his brother and makes it to his seat, I can't help but wish he'd get beat more often. Most days, he's there and hits me on the way by. The driver always says hey, does little more, anticipates nothing.

So every night when I go to bed, I listen inside the swell of the cicadas and actively hope to hear Justin shouting out. I don't even feel bad about wishing for it anymore. My parents never seem to care. I just assume they don't hear it. I do, sometimes, but I still pray for an empty driveway the next morning as I fall asleep.

I'm watching your backpack swing on your shoulder. I wonder when we'll stop and empty it out, take a look at it all. You're fast, but there's a sagging gait to you. It's really more of a trundling than a stride and I keep close, or as close as I can.

We take off out those woods that let out into a just-tilled cornfield. A few hundred feet away, inside a dusty cloud between us and I-80, a combine turns, then spits corn out a chute into a trailer. Some cobs spill, get left behind. You bend over, pick one up, chuck it. It caroms off the crenellated grooves of the earth, shoots up high. I lose it in the sun.

We walk around out there for a while. Our steps are hard, unpredictable. The ground trips us up, looks huge, like the baleen of a whale. We lurch across it to the road. We head down the hot blacktop past those abandoned aluminum buildings you like. They punch occasional holes in the woods that run along both sides of the road. You tell me how they used to be small industrial workshops, places to buy panels of marble, granite. Your voice tries on the tone of a teacher, but those places are nothing now. The walls of them wilt like lilies and the sun is so hot that it leaches black beads of shine from patched cracks in the asphalt.

You dive away from 6, down a ditch, into that concrete culvert that runs back under the road.

You told me once when your parents were still alive that your dad liked to say that strong leaders never check to confirm that you're following them.

Now you say that all the time.

I'm at the edge of the culvert, and from the road above, it looks immediately endless and hopelessly dark. When I go inside, it isn't. It's musty and cool like a basement, but the light fills the culvert fairly easily. You're halfway down. You have your pack sitting on the high side of the floor, out of the shallow section of that stream that passes through there.

I stop when I get close to you and see that you've got pages of naked girls under your arm already, a roll of masking tape around your wrist. A ragged Playboy sits open on your bag. It's mostly words by the time I see it, but twenty or thirty feet of the culvert wall is covered with these girls. I see their bodies. I see everything, actually. They're everywhere. I put on that it's no big deal, wonder how long you've been going there.

You hand me pages, tape. We take some time to put them on the wall. The cold concrete seeps through the masking tape, leaves a slick film behind.

It's the skin on their hips, though, that attracts me most. It's all so blotchy and tan lined, almost like the hills of a desert from the sky. I try not to fixate on their breasts, everything else, but for a second. I think about this bath my mom gave me when I was really sick. I'm embarrassed that it's what I'm thinking about, shake it off, study those things a bikini shows. I look at their eyes, their hips, and then those hollows beside their necks. All their mouths are open just enough to see a bit of their teeth. I settle into that.

But you look at me.

You have a placid face when you aren't smiling, inquisitive. It's your static face.

My static face is a smile. I don't particularly like that, but it's what I show you anyway.

"What?" I say.

"You like that?"

"I like what?" I say but know you mean the girls.

You chortle, don't respond. You rumble in the shadows, and we're forever there. I wait for you to say it's okay to go, but before you do, you grab at your crotch again, rub at it, stare at the pictures for a minute. At first, I watch you, almost study you, and then I don't and look away. I'm still trying to ignore you when you take off out the culvert and down the stream, leave the pack behind. I watch you lumber out into the light and then you're gone.

I hurry out.

Coming out of the culvert and into the sun, the musty air gives way to the bright tang of ditch flowers and the exhaust from a couple of trucks. Behind us, the trucks wail down 6 on their way to that new landfill by Starved Rock.

Your shoes are still on as you splash away from me, through the stream. It's ankle-deep where you are. It doesn't slow you down. I rush up behind you. The water fights me and I push through it. But you tread deeper. You look like you're dragging a tackler. The water's at your knees, my waist, and we stop long enough for you to tell me about how Stephen King, in Stand By Me, goes on and on about how leeches like to go for the dick and balls.

You take off again into the river, start to laugh.

"Watch the cock and balls," you say over your shoulder.

I laugh at this, but soon we're a ways into the stream. An hour in, it's really more of a muddy river. It's pushy like one, and we talk about how we can no longer see most of it.

"If we floated around in this long enough," you say, "you know we'd end up in the Gulf of Mexico, the Mississippi Delta?"

The idea excites me, but even though the river's just a shallow leg there, it's already all around us and everywhere. Trees are taken by it. Their roots cling to the shore, but they lay in the water. Their branches are laced with plastic bottles and bags. We pass a tree: dead, gray. Inside its limbs, duck down spins on the surface of the water.

But you're checking on me. Whatever your dad used to say aside, you turn to me and seem to override it, because you ask how I'm doing.

I'm okay.

You fall back, wait for me, tread alongside. Through my jeans, as we continue on, I can feel your legs whoosh in the water beside mine. I don't need to see myself to know that my eyes are big and open when you check on me again, the river chest high now, and you wading to the side.

We rest on the shore.

"Check your balls," you say, smile.

I say nothing, just look at you.

"For leeches," you say, and I do, look down my pants.

You look too.

"You're okay."

Still out of breath, you smack my back. It cracks like a firecracker and you're off again. You pull at the back of your shirt to take it off and it tries to stick to you, gives way. You tie it through a belt loop as you hit the river line, stomp through sedge grass, plop into the water, disappear, reemerge whooping.

We're in that river until it's up to my chin. I look toward the sky, and, still, water occasionally rolls over my lips and into my mouth. The clay in it stings when it splashes into my eyes, but I don't say stop because it's you. I trust you, want to be near you, am having fun, and it's a halcyon wind that's over the river. It simply passes like a ghost between us. It's, honestly, beautiful, and with your hand skimming the surface, your waist barges through the river like a head log.

I monitor you out of the corner of my eye because I'm tired. I paddle beside you as long as I can until the river outstrips me, bucks off toward Mississippi before us and into the Gulf. My fingers wobble through the current. I try to right myself. The toes of my shoes drag the river bed, tap at the bottom like for something missing and you grab me, say it's time to head back, ford me to shore by my arm.

Back at your grandma's, we take our soaked shoes off, sit on the deck in the late afternoon heat, suck down Cokes, and you get up, go inside, come back out with a driver and a box of golf balls, tees. You're sliding tees between the boards of the deck, driving balls deep into the woods when my parents come back for me. I throw my shoes back on, hop in. Pings off the club fill my parents' car as Dad waits for traffic to clear on 6. Mom's talking about work. I turn and watch you take another swing. A thin streak of white shoots skyward. A tee fires into the yard and Dad pulls out. We head home, the seams of my jeans still wet. I shift uncomfortably in my seat, roll up the window, slide between my parents and onto the console. The cold from the air conditioning feels so good my mouth falls open.

"You have fun?" Dad says.

I did.

That night, Honeymooners comes on and I still smell like the river. Mom falls asleep on the couch. Dad tells me to take a shower and I fight him on it because I don't like showers, can't stand baths.

He sends me to bed.

I'm asleep and wake up to the banging around at Justin's next door, shouting.

I go to my window. Their curtains are closed. Glass breaks. Justin's mom yells at him and his brother. More things shatter and Justin sounds like he could be in some pain. A shadow cuts fast across the curtains. Then his mom screams out too. Justin's brother tells them both to fuck off so loudly I can hear it with the window shut.

"Dad?" I say. "Mom?"

"We're up," Dad says.

The foyer lamp comes on. Light creeps into my room under the door. The dog's tags ring in the hall.

"Go back to bed," Dad says.

I can't and listen for a second, get up. I open the door to Mom and Dad. They turn the foyer light off, go to the front window, look next door. Dad's got the dog by the collar.

"Go back to bed," Mom says too, doesn't turn to me. She's petting the dog, still staring out the window.

"Should we call someone? I mean, should we call the police?" Dad says.

"Maybe," I say.

"No," Mom says, turns, puts her arm around me. "It's none of our business. Come on. Didn't I ask you to go to bed?"

Dad sees that I'm not hustling off and he scowls at me for it, tells me to listen to Mom. I go to my room, slam the door shut, rush to my bed, cover up. I can hear the dog sprint back to my parents' room through the hallway wall, jump onto their mattress as I close my eyes. I fall asleep to Justin's family arguing. It escapes their house, reaches across their lawn, and consumes both of mine.

A few days later, I'm on your porch, and your shoes are still there. They're curled up, heavy with cracked mud. You yell from your bedroom window that you'll be right down. I sit on the steps, watch squirrels chase each other around the oak you helped me bury wheat pennies under because I thought they were rare. The morning's cool because the sun's behind the trees and it's rained. You come out and the screen door slams. You put your shoes on, snake your foot in. It shakes the porch.

"I never noticed how the road is higher in the middle," I say because of dark pools of water that have collected in long ribbons on the blacktop.

"You see how the rain's still in the low spots?" you say and I'm staring at it when a truck howls through one, sprays water from 6 that explodes like waves against revetments.

"Yeah," I say.

Across 6 there's that place, The Riverside Pet Shop. We cross, go in. It's green everywhere and smells like bird shit, wet cedar. The fluorescent lights are tucked into the corners of the ceiling. They create a steady but scouring light. Like a pool at night, the center of the old store is dark. I avoid it. Next door, dogs bark through the walls of the neighboring vet's office. It seems to scare the birds. They're like bees in a bag against the wall. Their wings batter their cages. They spill their water, run into one another.

You're bent over staring into a glass case. Your hair keeps falling out of the ponytail you wear because of Swayze. You pull it back, tuck it behind your ears. On my way to you, spiders hide under artificial forests. A cat glares from a counter.

"Can I see it?" you say. "These are, what, ball pythons?"

"They are," the owner says. "This one's about one or two years old. We're not exactly sure, but somewhere around there."

The owner reaches into an aquarium, comes out carefully cradling one of two golden snakes inside. His hand is hard around the back of its head, but gentle, like he loves it. It's pretty clear that he does. It swings around his arm, wanders up it. It looks heavy and long like the wet beach towels my dad walks around the house with, calls a rat's tail. He bursts into my room from time to time and flips my lights on and off with them.

The owner hands the snake to you. It eases itself around you. This makes you smile.

I'm not, because, under a blown speaker spitting out Pop, what I am is scared of the thing: the weight of it in your hands, how you say it's heavy and cold, but dry, beautiful. I back away from you when you turn to give it to me. The owner says it's okay to put some money down on it. You do, beam, but your features bleach out in the harsh fixture that hangs over the counter.

When you push open the door to go back outside, we're blitzed with yellow daylight. The sun's come out. It's gotten hot again. You hop off the steps in front of the store, stand in a small patch of grass, pick at your nails, look bored.

"What you want to do?" I say.

You're grinning and soon we go back to your place. You still seem high from the shop, ignore me for a while. I feel like I'm bothering you, wish I had my Nintendo, try to remember to bring it next time. Your grandma's Cubs rise up through the floor. It's clear enough to know it's a 3-2 game. You complain about the volume, shout at your grandma without even leaving the room, but it changes nothing.

I'm sitting quietly on your bed for what feels like a long time. You read Lord of the Rings. I watch the clock, stare at the walls, the cover of the book, the drawing of Gandalf. A hobbit over Gandalf's shoulder looks fat and terrified.

But looking at the book makes me think of my dad. I think of the way the leather couch smells where he forced me to listen to a record we checked out at the library of

The Hobbit. Then I just want to see him. I go to the window and look down [6] to see if he's there.

He isn't.

"Check this out," you say, toss your book on the bed. It bounces on the mattress when you jump off, lands on the rug.

I watch you tear apart your tape case, jerk around your stereo. You take a tape out, smack the buttons, slam a tape in.

"Glass Tiger," you say, press play.

I close my eyes and listen. I can feel you standing next to me, the warmth that falls from you, but the sterile bass crackles your speakers. You turn it up anyway. The production's hermetic yet energetic inside the flat, mid-range whispers of the rolling tape. I'm watching the white reels turn. You bob. I bob. We dance in your bedroom. It's fun to watch you. You shake the floor, rap your fingers on the bureau along with the music's simple time, turn, pretend the edge of the bed is a synthesizer, rock the solo. You're stomping along with the band, and by the time the song ends, I'm singing the chorus. I'm hot, take my shirt off and as the refrain fades, you fade too. You sink onto the floor beside your bed.

I sit next to you.

You jump up.

I worry it's me that made you do it, but I don't think it is.

Another day ends up near the river.

We're in those concrete overflow channels that follow 6 and keep your house from flooding in the heavy rain, cut the woods into parts. We've been walking a while in those channels and I'm ahead of you. Behind me, you're fumbling around in your backpack.

I stop and you shoot a look at me.

"Keep going," you say, shoo me along with your hand.

I keep going.

Eventually, you stop and I come back to you. When we sit on the edge of the woods in the sun, I sweat into my eyes and you show me why we've come so far out away from your grandma's.

The book you brought is filled with these drawings of two naked people. One's a skinny Huey Lewis. The other, the girl, more nondescript, has hair like everyone my parents know. Her curls are loose and long, and big. In the illustrations, she's transparent. A golden bracelet glows through her arm. Her defining feature: no insides, barely there. You keep turning, narrate, turn another page, and he's inside her. This is where you stop, smile at the book.

"I can't believe you can actually see his cock in her," you say, laugh, look down at me. Your face is open and wild.

I look away. A canopy of oaks and elms splatters light on us. 6 is pretty far. Still, I can see a car pass. The silver car flickers between the trees on the edge of the woods and is gone. It was barely believable while it was there, strobing by like a flipbook.

But my eyes come back to you. Your hand's between pages. You go to say something to me, don't, linger on the images instead, your mouth still open. Your tongue lolls on your lip like smoke. You do this for a while.

So, I do too, until you close the book, slip it back into your bag and we cut through the woods in silence, head back to your place. Your grandma's in her chair, lost in a snoring jag. We go upstairs. I sit on your bed. You play your Glass Tiger, take the book out of your bag, open it up next to me, stand over it, leer into it.

At first, it seems like you're reluctant to, but something must give way in you, because I'm looking up to you and you undo your belt without so much as a visible pause to consider me. Then you undo your jeans, pull down your underwear. You put your cock in your hand. You almost talk to me but start to masturbate. With one hand holding open the book, your jaw hangs, your mouth black.

I don't really know what to think, what to do, don't actually comprehend you fully, but I don't leave either. Instead, I sit on the floor near you, focus on the cover of the Lord of the Rings book that still lies next to your bed. Somewhere, I'm reaching for a ring resting in silt at the bottom of a cavern, putting it on. But there, I don't do anything but manage to watch you for a second. Then I just try to ignore you.

But the bed squeaks and you stop, stand up. You're only a couple feet from me, still kneading your cock in your hand. You pitch over me, a skyscraper in Chicago.

I'm attached to the floor, still, quiet, and find your eyes.

You look at me looking up at you, then pull up your pants, walk out, leave.

I don't touch anything up there: your stereo, your comics, nothing. The window's shut and it stays that way. Sweat runs down the inside of my arm and I go out of my way to notice nothing. Light: just a vagueness, a happenstance of existence. But I want you to come back. I believe that it will answer something, make something easier for me, but you don't. I watch for you down the hallway, want to say I'm sorry, but don't know why and don't get a chance to know.

The tape ends, clicks itself off, and you leave me in your bedroom until it's time to go home. I'm still where you left me when my parents come to pick me up. Gravel sputters under their tires outside.

When I leave, you don't say goodbye. You're sitting on the couch in the living room. Your grandma's still in her chair and tosses this half-assed salutation my way, but you just sit there, ignore me. I leave, wave at the house from the car, its windows vacant, and ride quietly home.

I say nothing to my parents about what you did, because I'm not sure what it was.

I'm not sure if I did it too.

But in bed later, I'm trying to fall asleep. My window's cracked. The hiss of the summer cicada pulses, pulses, pulses, fades like some distant missile that never comes down. My neighbors are fighting. It's keeping me up. I shut my eyes, commit to not opening them until morning. Still, the red of the alarm clock seeps in, and with Justin and his brother breaking shit again, screaming at one another, my parents mumbling in the next room, I work to ignore it all, try to masturbate for the first time.

I'm thinking about the transparent girl. I'm thinking about the girls on the culvert wall, but fall asleep, a fleece blanket wrapped around my limp dick in the dark.

And then hysterical red and blue lights spin.

"You up?" Dad says through the wall.

I am, my arm numb and under me, asleep. I'm on my stomach, sheets on the floor and ass-out naked.

"I'm up," I say, go to my window.

Next door, there's cops, an ambulance. Justin's brother is in the back of one of the cops' cruisers. His mom sits on the driveway next to a statey. His dad comes back from work – he works swings – hops out, leaves the car running, the headlights on. The cops hold onto him when he tries to run at the ambulance, then the car with Justin's brother inside. He kicks the back door of the cruiser, fights with the cops. They push him to the ground, then help him up, usher him over to Justin's mom. He gropes at her, tries to get her in his arms. He fumbles for her, but she doesn't move at all. It's like he isn't even there. It's more like he never was.

I throw some pajamas on, go downstairs, and my parents and I stand in the foyer in the dark. We watch it all for a bit. The cops turn most of their lights off. Some start to leave. Justin's brother is shouting something from the back seat of the cruiser. Mom's robe smells like lavender. Dad puts his arm around my shoulders, pulls me close. The ambulance slowly backs into their drive. The dog barks at it but hides between my legs. Dad hollers at him and he stops, whimpers. Mom kisses me on the head.

About ten minutes later, everyone's running around again next door.

"Jesus," Mom says, clutches for me.

Dad and I say nothing.

I pet the dog, scratch behind his ear.

Justin's brought out in a bag.

It's morning. Dad knocks on my bedroom door, says that we have to go, that we're late. He's being really nice about it and I pop up, throw something on.

I don't know what to expect when I see you. I pack up my Nintendo, bring it with me. You're in the garage putting your clubs away when we pull into the drive. It's raining. You run from the garage to the house. I've never really seen you run at full speed. It's a sight. You're clumsy, bulky, a rhino being chased by poachers.

When my parents leave, it occurs to me that I don't want to go inside the house with you. I'm unsure of what to think of you, don't want to spend the day indoors, but with the rain wailing on the roof like suppression fire, I know I'll have to.

And we do.

You help me set up the Nintendo in your bedroom and we play Mario all morning. It's all regular. We sit on your bed, do the high fives, get pretty far in the game. You make us a Jack's, bring us up drinks. I'm happy. And you seem happy. We play through lunch. We smell like grease, and our slices hang from our mouths as we jump for flagpoles, chase coins, battle spinning Bowsers. Whole Toto albums come and go. We go downstairs, watch a

Cubs game with your grandma, go to Riverside, pay for the rest of your snake.

You bring it in. I take an end of the aquarium on the way up the stairs. We struggle to keep it level and the python slides toward me. The weight shifts. I almost drop him.

"Watch it, man," you say sharply.

"I'm sorry."

"Knock it off," your grandma says from her chair and we do.

"I'm sorry," you say and I bet you are.

When we get to your room, we slide the ghetto blaster off your bureau, put the python on. You feed it a dead mouse. It moves through the python's body like breath through a balloon.

At no point do you ever say anything about the last time I was there. I don't bring it up either. The day just passes. I go home, try to forget about whatever had happened between us, but I don't.

I'm at your place again, weeks later, the summer ending, the last day I see you, and it all starts with the porn. I loiter far behind you now. It's a building fear of you I feel, but I follow you anyway, down to that culvert.

I take the girls in this time, their bodies now part of me. Some of them have fallen on the ground, their pictures pulp. They float down the stream. Their faces slip away, are stunned white when they reach the sun. There's an urge to chase them, though I'm not sure why. I've come to love them, these women, in some weird way. Or, at least, it feels like love to me. But standing there in the culvert, the pictures, the girls turn to mush, and I simply want to save them. I want to save the girls from destruction of some kind, from the noise of youth. But I know I can't. I even know that no one really ever can.

So, we hang out, wander around for a while, end up in the woods, inside that foundation. I sit on the edge of it and cringe when you pull out that book with the empty girl in it.

I decide I want control of it instead of you, so I ask to see it.

You let me.

I flip through it like I'm teaching you to read, and you lean in.

In what is just a few seconds, I can feel you collapse into me. I turn to you, and in some kind of hurry, your belt is already undone. You're smiling. Not at me, but past me, at nothing. You're talking again in those terse, quick sentences and I can almost see you coming out of some shell you believe you have to come out of. You jerk at the zipper of your jeans, your underwear, and start to masturbate again in front of me. This time, though, you try for my hand.

I pull it back but stay put. I'm on the damp floor of the woods now. I can feel the cool of it soak through the knees of my pants and you're over me.

You grab at my arm, get it, pull me toward you. You lift me a little off the ground and set me next to you. You get yourself hard with one hand, press me to you with the other. The hair on your legs pushes through my shirt.

I just turn away.

But I'm close to you, and with your hand over mine, you wrap us both around you. It's a haunting warmth I feel in my hand, and you squeeze it for you, squeeze it again and again as I look off, try and keep my eyes closed.

The cicadas wheeze all around us. It's them I focus on instead of you. I memorize everything about their rattling as I'm kneeling there on the ground. They sputter like sprinklers.

But maybe it's the gray ghosts of the radium girls, because, for just a moment, I catch you distracted. You stop and I pop up, take off.

You don't follow me, but I still run from you. Somewhere inside me I continue to believe you won't chase me, so I stop, turn on a ridge.

You're standing alone in that clearing. You pull up your pants, turn away from me. Shadows are over you. You're lost somewhere in them.

I'm standing on the ridge in the woods watching you and I don't know why. I feel sorry for you and I don't know why. Again, I feel this need to apologize. It's overwhelming.

"I'm sorry," I say, even though I don't think you can hear it.

You're all exposed. You look confused and I wonder if you were trying to share something with me, figure you must have been. But I'm out of breath, out of there.

When you take a step in my direction, I run all the way back to your place, stumble up the porch steps, go in. Your grandma says hi to me. I say hi to her – a reflex, I suppose. I'm angry at her and blame her for you, but I head up to your room, open your window, lift your python out of the aquarium, toss it out the window. I hear it hit the bushes outside.

It was heavy. It was cold and dry, beautiful.

I take as many of your comics as I can carry, run back down the stairs, head out the back door, hide behind the garage until I see you wander into your yard, go in. When you do, I sprint across 6, wait behind the vet's, hide for hours, but I'm too afraid you'll spot me to monitor your house, or to look for you looking for me.

I stare down 6 toward town as the sun falls away. Eventually, my parents' Pontiac shows, emerges out of the buildings. I watch my parents turn onto 6, rumble over our culvert and toward your house. I watch them until they almost pass by me before I come out of hiding, wave from the steps of the vet's, jump up and down so they'll see me. They do, pull in, ask where you are when I get in, toss your comics into the footwell. I say you're inside.

And you are.

But that night the moon is out and I genuinely like how it seeps into my room through the blinds. Bars fall over me in bed and the Honeymooners is on downstairs. The cranked-up audience laughter has been reduced to a hum through the floor, a susurration through the vents.

I lay there. I'm still and quiet, my eyes open. The ceiling's a gray nothing. I sweat, am wide awake, and sort of stow away inside myself, put things in places, you in places. But I can see you standing in the woods. I put it away. I watch you from that ridge, your standing there, put it away. And in the dim of my room, a fan still spins, but there's some part of me noticeably already changed.

Cicadas hiss everywhere outside. They sing for each other in the dark, then pierce their exoskeletons, abandon their thin shells to cling to trees. Their shells only float away once the wind picks up real heavy, sweeps across the county acres. Before that summer ends, Mom and Dad take me out back where we retrieve their hollow bodies from the crevices of the shagbark hickories in our yard.

I eventually fall asleep listening to the rut of those cicadas, then wake up the next morning, go downstairs to the kitchen. Dad's picking bread from the toaster with salad tongs. Mom's got four boxes of cereal in her arms. The dog is sitting on the rug, looks warm in the electric sunlight from the window.

We eat breakfast.

I lie. I lie and tell them that it was the cicadas and not you that kept me up all night.

"They're magicicadas," Mom says, clumsily trying to unleash some ancillary wonder upon me. "They go away. Once it stops, you won't hear that sound again for a long time."

Dad clangs a spoon around in his bowl, ladles some milk out, feeds it to the dog under the table.

"The 'magic' is that it takes thirteen years for those things to come back. That's their trick. You'll just be outside someday and it'll all come back to you," Dad says and that's exactly what it did.

It all came back.

•

The following Monday, school starts up.

It's that loitering, Indian summer hot and I'm waiting for the bus, listening to the Walkman my parents got me. This black plastic Jedi backpack I begged my parents for makes me sweat a line down my back, but Justin's driveway is clear.

Through the blur of heat rising from the blacktop, the bus comes glistening down 6 and I get on. With Justin's seat empty, I smile. I just grin at the vacancy as the door collapses shut behind me. I drag a hand on his brown vinyl seat as I pass it, keep looking over my shoulder as I go all the way to the back, to Stills' spot. I pull those spring-loaded levers on the window. They clack as I let in some air, plop down on what feels like a cruelly hot seat. Then I turn up my music, turn up my KISS. Kids play in their seats, take toys out of their backpacks and my smile fades. As the death of not just Justin, but two boys, begins to sink in, put its hands on me, shape me, the bus crosses over our culvert on the way to school, and I ignore everyone while Destroyer fractures small bones in my ears.

ORCHID HOUSE

"An air plant."

"A what?" I said.

"An air plant," she said.

Al let her jaw hang open. Through the patina of the greenhouse, I could see the sun, a ruby through her cheek.

"You see that?" she said. Her hand drifted along like a boat would. Leaves spilled out of these air plants growing in trees. "They're so beautiful."

"It's the smell I love," I said.

"I know," she said. "It smells wonderful in here."

We stood together in the humidity of the greenhouse at the Lincoln Park Zoo. We found a variety of orchids there: the white egret, the moth. Sweat collected under our shirts.

She leaned into me. Her narrow collection of lines, her breath on my chest, our first moments alone together spent quietly under faint green panes of leaden glass.

A guide passed.

"The architect wanted this place to feel personal, like you owned it," the guide said. She had an old guy by the elbow. An old woman trailed, leaned into the words of the guide, clutched for the old man's jacket.

"See those glass panels? See how they open up?" the guide continued. "He hung them himself. He said they would refract light, that they would keep the temperature in here a more consistent degree. The plants like it, but I think it's a little hot."

The guide led the older couple around a brick walkway. Her hair fell out of her pins. She held a handful of it as they all walked out under an ivied arch.

"What'd she say?" Al said. "I couldn't hear."

"She said the guy who designed this place was thinking about light through glass," I said.

She slid her hand down my thigh. I grabbed it, searched for the bones of her fingers with my thumb. There was no part of her I didn't want to know.

"Earlier I said 'home' and you said nothing," I said. "I take that as a good sign?"

She said nothing.

Then, she brightened.

"Yes," she said. "It's a good thing."

A small, white flower grew above a koi pond.

"Hey, a ghost orchid. Right?" I traced the flower with my finger in the air. It was a ski jump covered in snow. I said so. "You see how you can almost see a tiny little Olympian shoot off the edge of it?"

"Yeah," she said, grinned.

Muscles on her neck flashed. I wanted to kiss them.

"Have you seen *Adaptation*?"

"No," she said.

"You know what I'm talking about?"

"No," she said.

"With Nicolas Cage?"

"No," she said, laughing now.

"Maybe we can rent it tonight?" I said.

"Okay," she said.

She spun toward the door. I followed.

While still married to other people, we'd once fed ducks and geese behind her apartment in Indiana. Because I'd just seen Sans Soleil, I asked if she knew that there were emu in the Île de France. She did. Such were the things that made us.

In the Orchid House, I thought about that instead of where we both had been before each other, what places she may have once arrived at, come from, without me.

I'd been so many places without her.

"Do you think swans know how good looking they are?" I said.

"Yes," she said. "You can tell."

I looked down her blouse. She caught me. Her eyes narrowed.

"What?" she said.

"What?" I said.

for Al

A PARENT
LIFE

Per our ritual, my wife and I come home from work one Friday night and meet in the kitchen to hold our cooking competition. Since neither of us ever want to cook at the end of the week, we'd agreed years back that we'd share the load, make a thing of it. So, under the bleaching of a fluorescent light, the sour whiff of Osage orange and the basil and cilantro she grows on our deck slipping through the cracked-open kitchen window, Jean and I put our blue, cast-iron pots filled with water on roaring burners. We draw out cutting boards and knives, set up measuring cups, ramekins, and timers, make an Iron Chef-worthy prep area out of our newly updated, $30,000 kitchen. Then we set the oven to 350, throw pieces of our work clothes on the back of chairs and compete.

"You're going down," she says.

She looks me right in the eyes. Everything I need to know transmits right there.

"Ah," I say, taking it all in. "My pretty adversary."

We're not allowed to face the fridge until we hit our timers. Each of us has twenty minutes to present our plates to the other. I judge her plate and she judges mine. If you need an ingredient stored in the downstairs mega-freezer for some reason and leave to get it, you lose (you'd be surprised how much you really had to fight the urge to make a break for an appliance you could store a couple of dead bodies in to go retrieve some inexplicably critical ingredient). Actually, if you leave the newly re-tiled area of the kitchen for any reason, you lose. If you yell at the other contestant (your spouse), or the dog, or at all for that matter, you lose. There's this Hungry Man Salisbury Steak dinner we have as an incentive in the freezer that awaits the contestant that loses so badly they don't even produce an edible meal, so needless to say, we're not eager to stray from the rules and get disqualified, which happens almost as much as actually completing the competition.

But Jean has a distinct advantage: she always remembers what's in the fridge and is, in this way, a lot smarter than me. Such stuff is beyond the frustratingly rigid limits of my memory, but she's also just a much better chef than I am. She looks in the cabinet and fridge and sees a meal. I've gotten better, but I usually see a bunch of things that I can't make mac and cheese with.

I have an advantage, too, though: she's pregnant, and, thus, a little bulbous, temporarily diabetic, and slow. She's gotten so much easier to beat as the months have gone on. And with her now just into her eighth month, a nicer person would take pity on her, but looking at her trying to tie a microscopic bow with the straps of her apron that can't make it around her twice anymore, we're laughing out loud and I'm eyeing another victory. I haven't lost in almost a month and am competitive enough that I've begun to take a sick pleasure in watching her eat so many TV dinners that, if our competitions were a nightly thing, I'd be a little concerned for the nourishment of the baby.

We don't tell our doctor we do this.

The competition works for us. It makes our Fridays bearable. Most Fridays, we do our thing, and afterward, Jean and I sit on our couch with Modern Family on, eat these largely experimental, often incomplete and ill-conceived dinners, adrenaline still buzzing our bones, our faces flushed with blood, but done with dinner and that much closer to going to bed.

We began this ritual some years after Dairy Leap died. Dairy was Jean's daring and camera-friendly yet fierce and intimidatingly accomplished mother. Her fingernail beds were so dried out from decades of sweating into thin latex gloves that they cracked and bled without reason or notice. She had this bright blonde hair that had been rendered brittle and broken from all the fussing with it on her long-running television show that aired on WTTW-Chicago. Dairy, something that always struck me as an obvious nickname, is a name that, even years after her death, is uttered by Jean most days. Her name peppers our conversations and its mention frequently shapes choices we make. But the nickname itself, as I'm sure you could partially guess, was acquired due to her using dairy products in almost every recipe she'd ever published in a string of fairly well-selling cookbooks. She died of a heart attack at fifty-nine. It was Jean who suggested the cooking as a way to remember her mother, but I've come to dig it.

Some nights, Jean and I rush through dinner to get to something else. To get Jean to appreciate those rhythms and patterns of the land surrounding Ottawa, the knitted acres of farmland, we often drive the frontage roads that track the interstate and Fox and Illinois rivers out of town just to escape the frequent oppression of the house, the radio up. I sing and flex my biceps when I turn the wheel in hopes of riling Jean. In my mouth I feel the higher, louder notes rattle my molars like playing foil on a comb, but I get light-headed, have to stop.

Jean seems to love me like that, my more bombastic ways. But the environment I'm in plays a major role. At home I'm expected to be still and much quieter. Singing or making a similar kind of racket isn't as welcome there as it is flying down the center of country roads. I suppose I know the reasons why this bothers her, though it doesn't always stop me from occasionally rousting the silent decorum from the house and stomping around in her PM quiet.

Sometimes, out driving, the wind will push us toward the ditch, like cattle in a squeeze chute, try to put us from the road. A country sky dark enough to look as though we're driving on the floor of the ocean will be everywhere as I fight wind, watch for deer that shoot from perforated edges of cornfields.

We can drive for hours like that, way, way out, past the rural grade schools that often look more like large sheds than a place you'd leave your child, past Pitstick Pavilion where there used to be a manmade lake and hilljack water park until Chad Doer dove in head first and predictably broke his neck. We drive out past where, at some point every summer, Jean and I plop a canoe into the Fox and slide downriver, passing fallen trees with owls and hawks perched on them and homes that range from sagging aluminum trailers to the historic houses that were there when Lincoln debated Douglas in Ottawa's Washington Park. The more we drive, the more familiar everything looks, and so, to me, it always feels like we're driving into time, into the steady past instead of something else, some other county, some other township or village flickering at night in the oft ignored but still proud and silently autonomous cultural margins of America.

Oftentimes we drive long enough to end up at the turn-of-the-century house Dairy spent her childhood at in Morris. Dairy had still owned the house at the time of her death and was renting it out. We almost moved into it when Dairy went, but, when you grow up in Ottawa, you grow up hating Morris, so I fought Jean on it, said I didn't want to live there and didn't want to deal with the upkeep. I have regretted it ever since. So we sold it and, with that money, Jean paid off the loans that she buried herself beneath to pay for the education her mother insisted she get, the loans Dairy asserted would help Jean appreciate how lucky she was to get into such a great school (Columbia University), help her to better "provide," as Dairy put it, for Jean's own kid someday.

We weren't sure we wanted any kids at all. On a lark, I eventually floated the idea when a cousin of mine had one, and Jean was clearly excited, so we started trying. Having lost the first two early, it took us three pregnancies we knew about, something we came to find out was pretty common, especially at our age. The one thing I knew about the whole thing was that it was going to be hard for us to have kids at all and, when we made it into that second trimester, one that felt very earned, when it was suddenly more certain, we bought all kinds of pastel shit for the kid and, indeed, started putting money away, just like Dairy had predicted. I was terrified, kept it to myself, and mined those places in me that were softening my stance on having a kid, that were bulldozing more and more of my being closed off to people and other parts of myself I fiercely protect.

Since I'm being honest, I don't like kids and I'm not interested in examining why, but for Jean, I'm learning to try, hoping that my feelings will change. Now that it's happening, it's Jean that wavers sometimes, something else we came to find out is pretty common, and I find myself buttressing her because I want her to have what she wants. No matter how she wavers, she always rights and I'm left trying to get to a place where, one day, I can be the guy she's hoping I can be.

Because, as of now, I need Jean for everything, was born broke, would still be broke if not for her. Jean is Jean: super competent, humblingly employable, and she ended up doing away with all our loans. But before all that and just after Dairy's death, what still remained of the estate set us up in Ottawa, afforded us a house much larger than we'd ever need. Still, we would drive out to Morris to see what the socially incompetent folks that Jean's lawyers sold the house to had done to Dairy's childhood home, which was nothing save for letting it sink into disrepair. We'd sit on the street and run up the cost of renovating it in our heads. It'd always been a bit of a hazy dream but it had recently started to become a real possibility.

Then, one Friday in early August, I'm thinking about all this, watching Jean shift her weight from side to side, while she and I stand in front of the fridge in our kitchen. Our hands on the counter, readying ourselves for battle, the dog anxiously poised to scavenge, Jean's face reads as though she's thinking hard, running down the list of items she knows are in the fridge and that she can throw together to bury me. Heat slips through the seal of the oven door while steam from the boiling water lazily lolls around in the hood. Jean swipes at the fog on her glasses, hangs them on her shirt.

"Okay," I say, "I'm ready."

"Yeah," she says.

"You look pretty," I say.

"Uh-huh," she says, rubs her leg. "You better focus."

Well into her early forties and even pregnant, most of Jean is still quite thin, just the way I like her, and just as thin as she insists I also stay. She's narrow, but not so desperately skinny and sharp you could count all her bones. The membrane on the wings of an ultralight, her skin's stretched over a visible frame, yes, but it makes her look purpose-built, fleet, and minimalistic, like something from a Mies van der Rohe sketchbook. Her eyes are large and often red from headaches and the computers that temporarily dull them at work, but the brawler in her flexes her slender arms to signal challenges that range from wrestling in the living room to what she is doing just then, flashing an ego-stuffed bravado in order to let me know I am about to lose the first cooking match I've lost in a good long while.

We had spoken on our way home that night about how Jean had had a bad day, how she and our baby were feeling, and I can see in the way she's standing there – the hair she's allowed to remain out of all her pins and clips, the way she's pinching her shoulder to momentarily fend off her migraine-inducing, mercilessly chronic tendonitis – that she needs to beat me. Seeing her like that, I believe it will take very little diving, but I still decide that I will, indeed, go down.

The timer buzzes.

I intentionally dump chopped onions onto the floor before sprinkling them into the pan. They dance in the heat. I lose dear seconds to it, while a paste is already coming together in the bottom of Jean's pan. She's whisking a roux, a hustler scrambling dice, and looks tiny and rabid, confident. I slow further, fumble for ingredients, allow her to take a greater and greater lead, and she visibly brightens until she begins to fade like an immature boxer. Because I am who I am, I seize the opportunity. I toss in mushrooms and red wine, spin a reduction in my pan, throw angel hair in rumbling water. Eventually, I dust her dinner with fresh parm just as the timer goes off.

Her entry's burned and inedible. It sits on the burner for some reason I didn't catch because I had accidentally found the groove. A pristine and wide-rimmed bowl gleams beside the stove.

"Get me the goddamned Hungry Man," she says, her belly pressed up against the burner knobs. Her hairline's damp and dark. Blonde strands stick to her cheeks. Sweat gathers in that nook beside her nose. She looks like she's been out in the rain, and, her being dinnerless, I step behind her, open the freezer, pull the pruny box of the Hungry Man out and slip her meal into the microwave without saying a word.

We sit.

She doesn't touch her fork.

I eat what I made. It's good.

She stares at me.

"What?" I say.

She just sits there.

"I'm not in the mood for this tonight," she says.

"Okay. What are you in the mood for?" I say, am immediately excited, know the mood she's in.

I love the moods, those moods where she's so unbelievably bored with something (with everything) that her personality falls apart, becomes wonderfully, wildly cumbersome.

Jean gets up, snatches the keys out the bowl and tosses them at me, everything still out on the counters, the table. Jean's by the door to the garage, impatient, crooked on a cockeyed hip.

I lock the dog up in the laundry room and follow her out to the garage. I feel that jolt of something electric in my bones when she gets that way, throws herself into the car, plugs in, syncs the iPod. She says nothing to me, yet to be married to her is to know precisely what a prize it is to give a night over to her without need of conversation, and I do.

Her belly in the way, she slowly wraps her seatbelt around herself. I see her being helped onto roller coasters, stuffing herself into the cockpit of some kayak, my helping her out of the tub. Once she's in, she's actually bouncing on the passenger seat, cradling her stomach with her arm, and she throws open every window as I turn the car over, back it out of the garage.

We're off.

I'm wound up and speed us everywhere. I barely watch for anything. I'm not careful at all, and Jean, too, is in this liberated state. I can feel her there, buzzing next to me. We cut through the country like a razor, and Jean just ignores the bugs hurtling into the windshield, something which usually sours her. She seems to turn up every song and I hang my hand on the damper that lines the moonroof, tug at my sleeves, pull hard at the wheel, flex for Jean. We pass a handful of country houses at high speed, pleasantly organic manure thick in humid air. Wallace grade school blurs by. Its white aluminum walls smear my periphery and, just beyond it, I don't know what I'm watching when I should be studying the ditches, but I accidentally confess a love for the music of Sheryl Crow, absorb this cruel look Jean gives me, and we're nevertheless singing "If It Makes You Happy" as loud as we can together when a few deer rush from the edges of the field.

I never make it to the brake.

The car bears downward as if going into deep water, howls. The windshield explodes onto us. My ears immediately ring. The huge and arching back of the deer consumes the void the explosion left. The deer's so close that even in the middle of all of it, all the shrieking of everything, I can smell the sour musk of its fur. It's right in front of my face. Pink skin lies under the tick and wire of its coat. But it's the sheer weight of the animal that drags the car to a stop, because when everything ceases its spinning, my headlights are staring straight into stalks of tall corn and we're left wrenched perpendicular to the field like a knife in the back.

The deer huffs short breaths between Jean and I. Like loose change, tempered glass trickles down the hood.

I can't see Jean, just the tortured back of the deer. I panic, call out for her.

Nothing.

I call to her again, still get nothing when the deer lurches, metal crumpling beneath its weight, stumbles off the hood.

The car dead, the deer wobbles in the ditch for a second like it's just been born and then tears off somewhere as I can now see Jean is totally out. There's blood in the pockets of her eyes.

I shake her.

I shake too when she finally moves, feels for her stomach. She says something I can't understand. Her voice crackles, a candle going out, and she deflates, air leaving a balloon.

"Baby, you hit your head," I say.

Nothing.

I don't know where my phone is, but I'm strangely and suddenly lucid for her, for the baby. I see Jean's purse emptied out in the footwell by her feet, grab her cell, call the sheriff.

Even way out where we are, they're poking at us in minutes. Emergency vehicles soon litter Wallace's parking lot. Colorful lights brighten the sky, a farm of wind turbines throbbing out red.

EMTs help Jean out the car, onto a gurney, me into the ambulance. The driver hits the siren and takes off as I strap into the bench across from Jean. She's in some kind of slow, delirious shock, but awake now.

"I'm here," I say.

She's pawing her sleeve at her eyes.

"I'm here."

The EMTs collaboratively work on her, monitor everything. They talk to each other, to her, forget me. Jean's eyes dark craters in her face, she stares off into things, through the walls of the ambulance. Her mouth's open. Her lips are dry, white, and I don't want to, but I think of dead babies, dead wives, of us, and she looks disturbingly pale, seems already lost on the gurney.

At the hospital, the EMTs delicately unload her from the ambulance like a live bomb, help me off. Just outside the ER, a doctor starts but immediately stops asking Jean questions. A bunch of people hustle her inside. She's quickly around a corner, just a streak of white and pale green.

I must appear passable. Nurses ask me questions, corral me into a chair in the waiting area of the too crowded ER. Finally, it's a doctor that sits me down, looks me over, and I cry, put my head on her shoulder. She lets me. I need her to, feel selfish, afraid.

"The nurses need your license and insurance. Do you have those things on you?" the doctor says. Even though my wallet's in my pocket, I tell her that I don't know where it is.

"I told her I have to be with her," I say, look across a crowded ER and stand up to try and push my way through it before I just settle back in my chair.

"Okay," she says. She pats me on my shoulder. "I'll let you know as soon as you can come and see her."

"Okay," I say.

I'm cold but give her my wallet.

Sometime during the night, that same doctor comes back out and tells me that they saved our baby. I cry again, this time from relief.

"And Jean?" I say, wait for the doctor to tell me that she saved her.

She never does.

•

When Dairy died, Jean and I were still at Columbia University, a place where one is simultaneously unreined to feel like a wild horse set free upon the world, and yet also saddled with enough debt to make you sometimes wish you were instead shot while still tied to a post in the barn. But, it was our time at Columbia and Dairy's death that became a part of what brought us together. Jean was broken up when I met her at the Lion's Head bar on the corner of 109 and Amsterdam. We'd taken this class together and got to talking after I had fought through this thick throng of graduate students and minor celebrities to get to her. This is what you do for a girl as pretty as Jean. And once you meet her, and get to know her, you'll cross room after room to get to her and for as long as she'll let you. I predicted this would be us and it was the first thing I said to her that seemed to register and she opened up, cheered up. I told her that, when it came to us, the too crowded room did not exist.

She believed me.

We talked for a long time at that bar, but at some point, she apologized, started crying and carrying on about how she wondered if her mother was actually proud of her. Then she apologized that she brought it up. In fact, it was a string of apologies from her, something rare in her now, thank God, since she and I feel that someone who apologizes a lot is weak and should be avoided/euthanized. It was clear that Jean's weak moment was rare, and also that it was never made obvious to Jean if her mother was proud of her at all, something I do think is important. Having just met her and it being about a year before the two of us started dating in earnest, I was who I was and tried to derail any conversation revolving around anything that didn't move her closer to coming back to my apartment with me. I failed.

But with her father long gone and both my parents gone too – I had lost my parents as a kid – this desire to make one's mother proud, even in death, which I know is strong in a lot of people and not unique to Jean, was so terribly strong that, like any gut wound, it slowly bled everywhere. But after we graduated and eventually got married, the cooking was such a logical tribute, we had to pick it up. Jean learned to cook to make her mom proud in some weird way that I guess made sense. At first, I was cooking for Jean, which to me also seemed natural, something I saw as a kind of marital obligation. It was only later that it turned into something that I ended up enjoying. But, it was who Jean and I were, what made us us that turned it into a thing, the thing being a competition instead of some sad morbidity we'd do better not to pursue.

After graduation, citing the asinine cost of trying to start and live a life in a chronically adolescent New York and the likelihood of our long-term financial instability there, we moved out and in with one another. We settled in Ottawa, the only place I'd ever lived besides New York City.

Ottawa's a place we believed could really use our presence, would actually notice it. Jean's not from Ottawa, but it's a welcoming spot, a valley township which sits in the depression of LaSalle County, and is surrounded by seldom interrupted square miles of soy and a god's reach of corn. Ottawa's world is populated by somewhere around 18,000 people, a couple of high schools, one private and Catholic, and one I was welcome at, a public one. There's a frail and failing Libbey-Owens-Ford glass factory, and a deep and ashy silica quarry that I know because of a Cessna ride an old classmate of my mom's had taken me on when I was a kid. Like any place, Ottawa's filled with a variety of other things that don't much make it all that special beyond the saccharine and the sentimental.

Unless you're from such a place.

Throughout my early childhood in Ottawa, I really knew very little sadness or loss. It wasn't until I was in high school that I went through some shit. Honestly, as much as I'd like to complicate the notion, as a young kid I was what most people think of when they think of Midwesterners. All I knew was switchgrass, baseball, M.J., and football, milkweed, how corn can snap at the bottom in a strong wind, and how farmers can lose big money to anyone from God to Monsanto if the weather is right. I knew that mice must populate every garage and attic in the world, and that that world is eternally quiet, especially at night when people are home for the day and you can take a dirt bike out to an I-80 overpass and into that classic, country dark to see how stars always disappear around the grainy edges of the moon as if lost in cataract.

Even romanticized so, some people go on the run. Dairy was desperately poor as a little girl, ran with kids that got her involved in fistfights and shit, and so ended up hating Morris and got out of there as fast as she could. Twenty-one when she moved to Chicago, she rented a place that overlooked the Ferris Wheel Restaurant, the Italian Village, an apartment atop a ragged stretch of State

Street at the time, and reveled in the city, eventually raised Jean near the lake there.

But flashes of Dairy's youth were left behind in pictures of her mother. Jean said that, when Dairy thought of her mom, what she was really thinking of were animated versions of the same three or four sepia-toned and cracked pictures, and a clipping the family had held onto from Ottawa's Daily Times. The clipping shows Dairy's mother hunchbacked on the job at a factory in Seneca that had a hand in making LSTs, the personnel transports used to bludgeon beachheads during the Second World War. She's grinning at the camera in the shot, but the way I understand it, she was almost always in pain and rode her bike from Morris to Seneca on those days she couldn't catch a ride to work. Jean said that Dairy told her that those real, more live-action memories of her mother, those ones that people try to make with their own parents so such a thing doesn't happen to them too, are not there for her to recall. Dairy said that what she really remembers of her mother is more like a cartoon than anything else. And that cartoon took place in a kitchen. So, the set Dairy cooked on was just that, a kitchen designed to closely resemble her mother's that she'd seen in some picture, and when I sometimes see Jean cooking along with one of Dairy's clips from her show on her iPad, it's hard for me to not see the scene sepia-toned too, see some golden version of Jean moving in an intergenerational, immutable animation.

At first in Jean's tiny apartment in New York and after Dairy had died and Jean and I had gotten to dating exclusively, like all people who mourn, I suppose, we would go through versions of various events and personality markers and make attempts to recreate them. We would watch episodes of Dairy's show on DVD, try to match her movements, spend whole Sundays going to claustrophobic grocery stores for baskets full of pricy, trendy filets of mahi mahi and enough heavy whipping cream to produce quenelle after quenelle with a wide range of consistencies and degrees of success. Some quenelles would hold their shape on a spoon and some would break like Brie left out at a summer picnic, but we would dutifully hover over Dairy's ancient food processor, tipping tablespoons of cream into it until we had gotten them to look as Dairy's had looked on the show. As you could guess, hers were right every time.

Sometimes, I would open Dairy's cookbook, flip through it page by page. Once I found a recipe for a pâte à choux and saw Dairy's handwriting in the margins. It read: "I've changed this J. It's now a half cup of egg whites and two tablespoons margarine. Feel free to change this to whatever your taste (and your health) dictates. It's the consistency that matters." Over the years, I read the "D" and the smiley face also drawn there as everything from a haunt and a tease to a genuine thing without the context of two lives attached to it, as if Jean were not Dairy's daughter at all but just another consumer with no access to the fights people have and the ways people apologize to one another. It wasn't until way later that I saw the missing comma between "this" and "J" as potentially intentional, as acknowledgement that Dairy had, indeed changed this very particular part of Jean, her desire to cook her mother's recipes, the part of Dairy she likely never intended to fully relinquish control of.

Jean said that she and Dairy had been fighting for weeks about how Jean's dad had remarried when Jean was young and that it didn't ever seem to bother Dairy at all. Perhaps informed by her dad's total disappearance after he got remarried, Jean said that she was nearly driven mad by Dairy's lack of emotion on the matter, that it was like nothing had ever happened between Dairy and her dad. She said that if something happened to us and I remarried that I'd come home one night to find my new wife had been murdered, and though she had been laughing at the time she had said this, it wasn't so obvious to me that she wasn't entirely serious.

Her dad getting remarried was something that Jean seems to have never quite gotten used to, but she said that she had wanted to apologize for how she was acting at the time and had made the bold move of cooking something of Dairy's for them both when Dairy had flown out to New York to visit her. She had spent the afternoon preparing the apartment she was worried Dairy would think was too small, was too close to Washington Heights, that Dairy would figure out that the Soviet-Block-style halfway house nearby had the same three or four folks in wheelchairs eternally smoking weed out front, one of them with a leg so beset with gout that it looked like turned kielbasa. This was something that Jean hadn't yet picked up on as a principal difference between New York and any other big city she'd been to: that New York apartments in a lot of the neighborhoods are so small and old that they never have central air. Their occupants spill out onto the stoops and the street immediately beyond simply to escape their homes and experience air again. The same scene in Chicago was usually a sign that you were in a neighborhood you should probably leave and Dairy didn't seem to notice much of anything else about the area, hurried inside. She ended up panning dinner, complained about the texture, started in on the importance of a final flavoring, and told Jean that it wasn't her fault, that she could show her how to fix it. And, Jean being Jean, she never forgot what even she would call a minor slight, never truly let it go, and I see it as something that eventually landed us in our kitchen.

Jean couldn't get to the hospital fast enough to see Dairy the day she died. Because I know how proud Dairy was and how she wouldn't want someone to see her so weak, I'm certain Dairy's dying alone bothered Jean way more than it did Dairy, but Jean told me that getting to Northwestern Memorial was harrowing. When a doctor called and said Jean should try to come back to Chicago to see Dairy, that Dairy was on bypass, Jean took a cab out of NYC in rush hour. She caught a flight into Chicago as soon as she could and took another cab into the Loop. Like everyone always does, she came in the wrong entrance at Northwestern, yelled at the hospital staff in the lobby trying to find out where Dairy was and then just yelled at anyone for anything. But by the time Jean got to Chicago, Dairy had already gone and Jean was so hurt by how long it took her to get home that I knew that I could never miss Jean's death.

She's just like Dairy. She wouldn't be scared either, but Jean believed me when I told her later that, like she had, I'd risk it all to be right there when she goes. I said this because I knew she'd do the same for me.

But, I guess I didn't.

Because she's so intolerant of posterity, wary of sentimentality, Jean wanted to cremate Dairy. Instead, she chose what Dairy preferred and had her buried in a grave in Graceland, up there by the house Jean grew up in near Wrigley Field, a grave we never visit.

My mom was second-generation from the Yucatán. A couple times a year she would wear this colorful, intentionally stereotypical ethnic get-up she'd held onto when her mom died in the '70s. Most of the time, she wore pantsuits and silk blouses that often still had pads in the shoulders to her job at the LaSalle County courthouse. Mom looked like someone companies send out to talk to the press or to calm rowdy protesters. She shared my big Yucatán face, and to conceal a tendency to frown whenever she wasn't smiling, she almost always smiled, looked like she was about to try and sell you something you'd eventually buy. Like me, my mom had what we called a Latin bump on the bridge of her nose, a knot that always held her glasses snugly to her face no matter the chore or activity she was involved in. She had this habit of not really listening to what you were saying and then fought you hard, stomped off when you got mad at her for forgetting to do whatever tasks of various importance she had promised to do. This inability to win with her, however charmed I might have been by it, was something that probably contributed to my dad leaving her and taking a job as a guard at the now-closed prison in Joliet where they filmed bits of The Blues Brothers. He continued to work there until he died of an aneurysm, collapsed in the intake office.

But, Dad was forgettable. As far as I know, he did not come into my room at night to make sure I was okay (it was Mom that did such things), nor did he ever let me ride on his back like a horse, loan me his Dylan records (Mom, too), or roll over me like a steamroller on the floor of our living room (Mom, again). Lord knows what he was really like, because he was gone well before I got to know him. He remains a cliché in my mind and, thus, not all that interesting to me. But he did leave me with red hair that curls like the Irish. I have to keep cleanly shaven unless I want to look like I'm from there, field questions about what I look like – something I'd never allow anyone to reduce me to without my spilling their blood.

For seventeen years, my mom worked at the courthouse as a clerk for a string of attorneys in the public defender's office. She'd seen dozens of either elected or appointed folks flow through the limestone building that sits by the river in Ottawa during her time. Like many of those in Chicago, the building sinks into the ground more and more every year. If you dig away from the foundation with your hands, you can see limestone blocks that used to feel the heat of the sun but are now forever lost to the damp of the earth. I've done it. I've placed my hands on the cold stone, but I imagined Mom doing things worthy of Hollywood films at work, and my visits to her traditional office only fueled such fantasies. We watched To Kill a Mockingbird together one night and I imagined her as some version of Peck, her playing a critical but thankless part in humanist and righteous victories waged on the floor of an oak-paneled courtroom. I imagined her to be unflappable and strong, something I believe she actually very much was, handing a lawyer this deathblow of evidence piece by piece that brought down some generic evildoer.

Mom would always start her stories the same way over dinners with: "Don't repeat this," but often followed it up with information I couldn't possibly appreciate the ramifications of at the time, like "Mr. Tamborini is a great lawyer, but he likes to go down to Allen Park to meet Mr. Durkus for lunch." These were gossipy statements I was too young to understand only for a short while. I caught up to their intended meanings by fifth grade but, being her only child and raising me alone, perhaps by default only, I ended up being one of the most trusted sources that she could vent to and have since treasured the role I played for her.

But then there were some people in Ottawa like George Hall, people who saw those single, sometimes widowed women like my mom as alone and vulnerable like some isolated pack animal exposed to being preyed upon. George worked with my mom at the courthouse, had gotten his law degree at Northwestern, thought that going there said more about him than it did. And for a while, the Mustang that was also nowhere near as magnificent as he thought it was would be in our driveway when I came home from school. Mom never remembered the days I was scheduled to get out of school early and my walking in on the two of them had gotten to the point where I made sure that I was always alone. I never had friends come over just after school.

For weeks I stepped off the bus, waited around in the yard, walked to 80 and back, did anything but go home.

But one day his car remained in the drive into the dark. I was furious and barged through the front door expecting a scene I'd built up in my mind, one filled with awful sounds that I no longer see as so awful coming from Mom's bedroom, something solely informed by movies, of course. But, I came in to see George sitting at our kitchen table. He had wide, thick lips, tiny ears. His hair was blowing around from the ceiling fan. He was wearing the same starched and navy papery suit he always seemed to have on when I'd come to see my mom at work.

"Sit down," my mom said, and I did. She put plates out for us, utensils, brought over dinner and we ate.

Afterward, George excused himself and Mom told me that my dad had died. She told me that he loved me and that he would miss me and I fell apart, gathered myself when she said that she was going to get George and that we had a small amount of money coming our way. George reappeared with paperwork for my mom to sign and she marked it up where he told her to. I watched her keep it together the whole time until after he left. Then we cried together on the couch, flipped through photo albums filled with pictures of me as a kid that I realized for the first time were live-action scenes that I'd built in my mind rather than remembered, and went to bed early.

At first, when Jean and I cooked, we would frequently have my mom's Betty Crocker and Dairy's own cookbooks out. We referenced them for a while, then tried not to use them as much, and then just Dairy's, until we eventually mostly abandoned the cookbooks altogether. I believed that they unfairly influenced me and thought that Jean didn't need the advantage they afforded her if the events were going to be fair. While the books at first ended up caked with chunks of flour and their pages turned wavy from having been soaked by oils, knocked over into sinks, they seldom make it out of the credenza in the corner of the kitchen now.

When we first started our competitions, I had no idea how to cook anything that wasn't boxed and Jean went on a streak of victories that was so demoralizing to me, due to having eaten Salisbury Steak for five straight weeks, that it was the one time she came home with other Hungry Man selections. I ate with tremendous joy and fervor Smokin' Backyard Barbeque, Grilled Bourbon Steak Strips, and I didn't even question whatever Mexican Style Fiesta was I was so grateful for the clemency she'd granted me. Another time I won six times in a row and she cited this mercy, but I grinned at her, turned to the freezer, held the Salisbury Steak over my head like Cusack's Gabriel-blaring radio.

Over the course of our marriage, we had gotten so steadfastly dedicated to our competitions that, one week in November, when the oven's burners just clicked because of a gas line that the root of a tree had grown into, the competition extended to which one of us could convince someone to come out and fix the line for us after hours. This was a competition she, perhaps not surprisingly, won. The guy came out, was in and out of the house so much that the temperature in the kitchen dropped to the point we could see our breath by the time he left. We resumed cooking. I won this one and we ate our dinners with stratus clouds streaming from our mouths.

•

More than anything, I want to look Jean in the eyes and assure her that I'll always be waiting for her, but Jean's brain swells and, even though the doctors drain the bleeding on it, drill holes through her skull, too much damage is done.

I'd done that damage. I feel the effects of having done it immediately and am crushed beneath it. Like Dairy, Jean dies somewhere deep inside a hospital without anyone she knows anywhere around. I sit in the horror of a waiting room knowing that, when I had promised that it would be different for her than it was for her mother, I had lied to Jean. This is all over my mind and continues to be in the weeks that follow Jean's death.

Worse, I try to forget that our baby survived. But, I can't. The doctors won't let me. They keep talking about it. Of course I know about this baby's existence in the world, but I don't care. I sit in the waiting room of the hospital repulsed by the only reason I can come up with to care about it at all: it had come from Jean. I'd rather feel parental but feel more distant from that baby than anything, living or dead, I've ever felt in my life.

The morning after Jean died, without saying anything to me about where we're going, Jean's doctor comes and retrieves me from the room security people had put me in after I fell apart in their waiting area, refused to go home, call anyone to be with me. The doctor comes quietly into the room that I've decided I want to die in, then walks me by the elbow to an elevator and out onto a floor where everyone's wearing pastel scrubs.

The first time I see Jean and I's baby, two nurses are hovering over it. They're changing its clothes. I don't want to see it, but there it is. It's an eclipse. I'd need some specially crafted device to look at it without causing permanent damage to myself, but like an eclipse, I look anyway. Through the nursery's window, I stare at it. Its writhing disgusts me. Even after seeing it, how vulnerable it is, maybe especially because of how vulnerable it is, it's simply just what is left of Jean. I don't want to see what is left. Out of my own guilt, certainly out of selfishness, Jean's the only thing I want to see.

"I don't want to do this," I say.

"Okay," the doctor says. "We can do it another time."

On our way back downstairs, the doctor and I wait for the elevator.

"I'm sorry, but I need to ask you something," the doctor says. "Did Jean ever communicate what she wanted should she – "

"She wants to be cremated," I say.

I never did understand how anyone could ever want that, why anyone would want to make someone set someone they still very much love on fire, but it's what Jean wanted and I have to do it for her. It kills me, but I have to.

"Okay," the doctor says. "There'll be some forms to sign, but I'll try to take care of as much of it for you as I can."

"Okay," I say, and the elevator door opens.

In a hospital office somewhere, I'm beat, flat broken down. I haven't really slept and am emotionally prostrate. I couldn't cry if I wanted to. A half dozen earnest folks make various suggestions and I try to appreciate them but can't yet. Someone says that there are programs for the widowed. There are groups of people who have gone through what I'm going through, and hearing this makes everything worse. First of all, I don't believe them. There just aren't that many people who lose the mother of their child, their wife, the way I did. Though it happens, it's not common. And second, heart attacks are common. Car crashes are common. But the obvious thing about that is, knowing that that's true doesn't spare you a thing. As people come in and out of the office to speak with me, I think about how, more than being simply justified, suicide makes sense, alcoholism makes sense. It sounds like the logical thing to do. I sit there wondering why even more people haven't killed themselves.

"Hello," someone says, coming through the office door.

"Hey," I say to what turns out to be another doctor, some therapist.

We talk about this and that and, eventually, like everyone else, he gets to the baby too.

"I'm going to broach a difficult subject, because I think it might be helpful to talk about it," he says. "When the baby comes home, you may need some help."

"I don't know, man. I don't know anybody," I say. "Our parents are gone."

"We can help with that," he says.

"I know," I say. "There are groups. I'm aware of the groups."

"There are," he says and hands me a pamphlet. He writes a number on the top. "Call this person in a couple of days. They're there specifically to help in these situations, and they do help."

There's a blankness.

I notice I'm shaking my head unconsciously.

"Okay," he says. "Let me know if I can do anything for you. I'll be by the nurse's station. Don't hesitate to ask if there's something we can do."

"Okay," I say and really just want him to leave.

He does. He nods at me for a few seconds and leaves the room, me to myself.

I look at the pamphlet, scoff.

Later, I'm told that the baby will have to stay in the hospital for a while and it does. Despite the doctors trying to find me some company, I walk out the sliding doors of the ER alone and take a cab home. I wasn't even aware that there was a cab service in Ottawa, but, standing in the parking lot as the yellow car swings around a corner and stops in front of me, I feel as low as I ever have. The sun across its roof, there's something so physical about the cab's presence that begins to distill crippling, amorphous pain in me. I go home without the baby, without Jean, feel completely alone. I come in the front door of a house I now hate, let the dog out of the laundry room he's peed and shit in. Like he always does, he runs around the house looking for Jean, and I cry in the middle of the kitchen as I watch his hope for her wane.

It's three weeks before I bring the baby home. Those three weeks pin me to more emotional pain than I could have ever imagined possible for someone to survive. Jean's everywhere. I believe I can smell her in the books I try and fail to read when I open them. I take in huge breaths of the bindings. She's every character. Movies I try to watch make me hear noises of her coming home from work that I know aren't actually there. The knowing is unique, and certainty never hurt so bad. Even the dog stands in the hallway waiting for her in a way I believe I've never seen before. He waits for her to come home for days and days until, about a week after the accident, I go to the hospital and bring her home.

"Yeah," I say, kneeling in front of the dog, crying, "it's Mama." He wags his tail at the mention of her name, sniffs at her urn.

I choose to interpret everything the dog does as his understanding something he probably doesn't, and, exhausted, I sit down on the cold tile of the foyer until he curls up next to me, puts his light chin on my leg. I can see his nose breathing but feel nothing at all.

I never thought of myself as a coward, but, in those three weeks before I bring the baby home, I first learn that I'm not brave enough to kill myself. I then learn that such an act doesn't factor in bravery at all. Aloofness saves my life every day. I blow out the pilot on the oven, let it run, forget about it, then come back to turn it off. I fill the tub, get in, even slip under the water, but then drain it, shower instead out of habit.

One night, I take out all the knives in the block and lay them out on the counter. Habitually, I look for Jean beside me wrapping her apron around her. Her absence makes me think of Dairy, then my own mom, and then, again, Jean and I cooking together, our battles. I put the knives back in the block. Thinking of our ridiculous competitions, I suddenly realize that, above all, what Jean hated in people was resignation. The desire to have the battles at all were, in many ways, a fight to spend more time together—the opposite of resignation, the opposite of apathy, the real adversary to any marriage, to any life. I stand in our kitchen, my hands on a cold, $8,000 piece of stone, and come to the conclusion that that could very well be the principal thing Jean loved about me. She loved that I resigned to no one, not even for the smallest stakes, not even for her.

I start to prepare to bring our baby home the next morning. The doctors help me figure out how to feed it without Jean, a thing that didn't even occur to me until they brought it up. I do solicit some help from a group of people who have raised a kid alone, single mothers mostly. The whole thing is awkward and arduous for me, but I focus on the details, really do want to make an attempt to get it right, though know I won't.

Despite whatever reservations I may have, I do start to see Jean and I's baby as the byproduct of how good Dairy, Jean, and my mother were, but I waste a lot of time trying to remember only the good things about them and hate how that softens their edges. If Anne, the name I'm finally able to give the baby, is to know them at all, she'll need to be let in on the bad as well, and, if I succumb to some resignation, I turn momentary pain into permanent trauma, make pain immutable instead of memory. I don't know who I am in those weeks, exactly. I'm right in the middle of everything, but I know I'm not someone who would do that.

I also know that I can't stay in our last house. I decide I'm going to finally buy Dairy's childhood place and start figuring out how to do it. I sit in front of the house in Morris, draft elevations and pencil in blueprint details in my head. With Anne on my lap, I spend a lot of time on the computer thinking about how I would want the place to look. In between Anne's diaper changes and random fits of inexplicable joy and cringe-inducing wailing, I go through photographs and videos while, all around me, stories organically emerge. Images place their hands on me, leave their fingerprints, and, through me, leave their fingerprints on Anne, too.

By the river in Morris, there's a pool hall where blown-out old folks sit at the bar in the middle of the day and eat dry hot dogs that have been swinging in a dimly lit rotisserie for far too long and drink Hamm's and Budweiser out a tap and plastic cups. High school kids skip and land there, play pool for hours as the staff makes no attempt to return them to the school-going population. The cracked and rolling-hillside-like concrete floors and sagging drop ceiling do nothing but more acutely fill in the gaps of detail missing from everyone's Color of Money-born fantasies. People have actually broken people's thumbs in the place, have done far worse, and have done so with regularity. I'd even been there when I was a kid, and, like every pool hall that's ever existed in the universe, it hadn't changed in decades. It was every bit a shithole, and, back when Dairy was in high school, this was the place she'd beaten some girl's ass.

Dairy was hanging out with this guy she was dating at the time when, like all high school problems, some sexually related bullshit popped up. The guy she was with had apparently been sleeping with someone else and that girl had come to the pool hall to find Dairy. When she did, she found Dairy and her guy with their backs both turned on their stools. The girl walked up behind Dairy, yanked her onto the floor by her hair. Dairy would tell this story unapologetically, had told Jean as some kind of cautionary tale Jean never could unpack, and the story went that Dairy got up swinging.

As Dairy waved missed shots at the girl, the girl ducked down and pushed her into the bar, backed up toward the door, and Dairy and her both got run outside by the bartender. Now a hockey fight, Dairy had the girl's shirt around her neck, was hitting her as hard as she could when the girl wriggled away, left Dairy with the girl's shirt in her hands, standing in the middle of the road. Girl ran off in her bra toward a chain-linked fence between them and a Tasty Freeze. Dairy chased after her, caught her, grabbed a handful of hair as the girl threw a leg over the fence. The girl kept going, dropped down on the other side. Screaming, she ran off with her hands around the back of her head, ducked into an alley in between the buildings and disappeared.

Dairy watched her run off with about a foot and a half of the girl's hair dangling from her hands. She ditched it, and the guy, too. She left him standing in the parking lot as the cops rolled in.

In a story that also necessitated the involvement of the authorities, Dairy'd once almost lost everything she worked for. She ran over a man in a wheelchair coming out of an alley in 1992. Setting it up that way almost sounds like the story's a joke, and it almost is, but she left her spot in the WTTW parking lot and headed toward the Loop via this narrow alley that runs along the side of the building where she shot her show. She did stop and honk as she pulled out of the alley, something that saved her jail time in the end, but hit the gas, and before she knew what was going on and could stop, Dairy felt and heard something go beneath the tires of this Cherokee she loved.

She did call the cops from her car phone but was so shocked, so scared, that she locked the doors and stayed in the car. As people surrounded her Jeep jutting halfway into the street, knocked on her windows and tried the doors, she carried out a conversation with the operator about how much she liked this building that was being built by the architect Philip Johnson.

"I hear there's gold leaf on the walls," she said.

"Ma'am," the operator said, "are you still at the scene?"

"It goes all the way to the ceiling," she said. "And the Lichtenstein that was in the Trib, that's supposed to go there – I never get over his colors. I love him."

"Ma'am?"

Nothing for a second.

"Would you look at that?" she said. "They're playing on the roof."

"Who's playing, ma'am?"

"They are," she said, talking about workers who had been laying copper roofing panels at the time.

"I could watch these guys for hours, their ropes hanging like the circus," she said.

"Ma'am. Are you okay? The police are already on their way."

Jean said they played the recording of this conversation in front of her and Dairy in a lawyer's office, a huge shadow of the Chicago Mercantile Exchange leaning across the table leaving Jean in the dark. Jean has the tape of the conversation in a box somewhere, and, later in the week, she and Dairy were getting the alignment on the Jeep fixed when Dairy was called out to the service bay.

The mechanic brought them out to upsell her, but the Cherokee was up on a lift. Its wheels hung, large fruit on branches.

"You could use some new front pads, but we can turn the rotors on the back, so you don't have to worry about that until next year or so," the mechanic said.

Dairy went a greenish white, a color Jean said she'd never forget.

"Just do the alignment and change the pads and leave the rest of the car alone," Dairy said, and Jean sat in the waiting area as Dairy watched the work through a chicken-wire window, paid in a hurry.

Dairy didn't speak at all as she drove them directly to a car wash. Jean watched Dairy get down on the ground to pressure wash the undercarriage of the Jeep. Wind blowing hair into Jean's mouth, light pink water slipped into the drain by her feet. Jean hid the stained shoes in her closet until, somewhere along the line, Dairy found them, unceremoniously threw them away without so much as a word.

Later, when Jean had told me this story, I had said to her that I thought it had to be blood that stained her shoes.

"You don't think I knew it was blood?" she said.

I had hoped she hadn't.

It was shock that caused the distant 911 non sequitur, the majestic nonsense, or at least this is the story the lawyers came up with and had been able to support in proceedings. Since witnesses said the man in the wheelchair ignored the horn and wheeled right in front of Dairy for some reason, she wasn't found culpable of anything, and seldom ever was. But Jean said Dairy spoke about the accident all the time, told it like an anecdote at parties, to friends and acquaintances, like something that had happened to someone else, and maybe it had. Maybe it had happened to that part of our personality that's able to deal with such things. Maybe it happened to the same entity that was dealing with my losing Jean as well.

I know enough to know that Mom, in the ways that count, was someone to emulate. She died young, of cancer, like a lot of people in my family. In the time between Cinco de Mayo and Thanksgiving one year, Mom went from black-haired, dark-skinned, and moody to timid, ashen, sub-100lbs, and with hair getting so gray and thin that she shaved it off just so the chemo couldn't take it all. I had a friend in the Army that had done the same thing. He'd gone to Mort's Barbershop, a small white house almost hidden on the back end of a funeral home's parking lot in downtown Ottawa, and shaved his head before he shipped off to Fort Leonard Wood, just to rob the Army of the pleasure, what he perceived of as some upper hand. And this was Mom. She didn't articulate it like that to me, but, like everything about her, you could see the obstinance, the rebellion in the expression on her face as she ran the Wahl over her skull.

"Help me clean this up," she said, and I did.

I stood behind her, crying. I took the clippers from her and hummed them up her neck, swiped over the tough, gray strands hanging on like weeds coming up through a parking lot.

I can still feel the buzz of the clippers.

"Thank you, honey," she said and brushed the clipper clean into the garbage can. She moved around the bathroom slowly, now spending much of her time afraid of falling, and swept the floor.

I watched her for a second before I ran the towel she had sitting on the sink under the faucet and tried to take the broom from her.

"It's okay," she said, refusing to let me take it.

I knew she wasn't talking about the broom.

Like all single parents, I'm sure, my mom was everything to me, did everything for me. She wasn't only a cook, but she was a cook. We'd spend a lot of time around the kitchen, too, just like Jean and Dairy – like a lot of people, I suppose.

"Get me another," Mom said one night while making us something to eat.

I fished a lasagna noodle out of the strainer in the sink. I sat one in Mom's casserole dish and went to watch the Sox.

"Do you, for some reason, think I'm going to do all the work here?" she said.

She was laughing, but I did.

The oven between us, she was in that place where she expected an answer. She tilted her head, slapped a spoon down on the counter.

"No," I said.

She stared at me, her hands astride the stovetop, until I began to get up to help, marinara steaming in a pot.

"Put on Channel 9 or turn it off and get over here," she said.

I did.

I put on 9 and helped make dinner. I quietly placed layer after layer of wide noodles into the casserole dish, heat from the oven releasing Mom's Aqua Net into the air.

Mom was all about this. Especially because she could, she wouldn't do anything alone. Because I think she saw it as an opportunity to teach, she always required my help. Like all kids, I had misunderstood this and her cooking for me most of my youth. I had misunderstood most things about her most of my youth, no matter how obvious they were once I got older. Mom was a teacher, a cop, a lawyer, a good friend, a judge and jury. She was the marker for all things and was all things, first because she had to be, and, even before Dad left us, because she wanted to be.

Two of the worst things I can remember Mom ever doing were still better than things I've done. We took the shitty car we had and went down to a car dealership on Ottawa's northeast side when I was pretty young. Everybody wore gray suits there, red ties. Even Mom had a gray suit on. We test drove a used '74 Firebird across town and, then, along the Illinois River, we were a copper bullet down Dee Bennett Road. She eyed me in the mirror, ignored the salesman talking about this and that. I remember the smile that cracked her face open when she hit the gas. I slipped from the center of the backseat into the ravine of the C pillar.

"What's going on back there?" she said. "Is your seatbelt on?"

"I don't know where it is," I said, and the wind came in through her window so fast I could feel it under my eyelids.

The salesman didn't even seem to mind when she didn't let up on the gas, until he did.

"You're going to need to let up," he said, laughing, but grabbed for the door so hard that blood was forced from his knuckles.

"Okay," she said, winked at me in the side mirror. "You win."

What was bad about this wasn't the drive, but how she bought the car and we only had it for a few months before someone took it in the middle of the day on a flatbed. Mom was standing in the drive talking to the guy with the truck and wasn't at all surprised by the whole thing. I know now that it was likely repossessed and that, Mom being Mom, was plenty smart enough to know that she shouldn't have bought it in the first place, but impulsivity was her impulse. To be honest, I don't think she ever planned on paying for the car at all. I never knew anyone that was quite so beyond credit, above it, or at least so able to avoid how most people allow it to dictate many of the decisions that shape their lives. I really don't think she ever considered it a factor of much of anything. How she reconciled what she did for work with that I don't know, but I really don't care.

Besides, when she was young, Mom had long been a bit of a kleptomaniac. At a family reunion once, she'd shrank from stories about her stealing insignificant things. Mom's cousin talked about how she used to shoplift records in high school.

"She was good at it," her cousin said when he must have thought I was too young to understand what he was saying.

"Stop," Mom said, laughing, everyone drinking, their arms stuck to plastic tablecloths in some family member's backyard.

"What she'd do was go in and ask for something under the counter and, when the guy went under the counter to look for whatever it was, she'd slide 45s under her shirt. It was so simple."

"Seriously," she said.

"She took whole records, too."

"Once," Mom said. "I did this one time."

She looked at me. BBQ smoked over a pit. Some distant cousin lit fireworks off in the street. Dogs barked at them.

"Twice," he said. "At least twice, because you got so bold that you knew what took the guy a long time to find under the counter and asked him for that, so you had more time. Didn't you also sell those records back to the store?"

"No," she said.

"I was with you when you did it," he said.

"No," she said, "I sold them some records I'd borrowed from a friend."

"For date money," he said. "Wasn't it?"

"For date money," she said, and everyone laughed. "What? He was cute. I wanted to go."

Mom shrugged, looked sunburned, maybe a little embarrassed, but didn't seem all that ashamed.

"So, I'm guilty of some minor offenses," she said. "Really minor offenses."

And she was.

"I'm reformed now," she said.

And she was.

The day she died had to be the sunniest of the year. She mumbled about the weather she could in no way feel from her hospital bed. I thought about death and she talked about life. Death was long accepted. It was air to her, had gone empirical. It hadn't for me.

It never really has.

I was trying to open a window for her when the nurse came in.

"You need a key for those," she said.

"Mom wants it open," I said.

"The blinds," Mom said, lifted her hand a little off the bed. "Blinds."

Sunlight was a band that went around the room, dividing it in half. Half of Mom was within it, under it, obscured by it; half of Mom was texture, a white, knitted blanket with the narrow ridge of her legs under it.

"I think she wants it closed," the nurse said and walked toward the window. "Let's see. Is that what you want?"

Nothing.

The nurse closed the blinds and I sat in the chair next to the bed as the room went from yellow sunlight to strident white, the fluorescents humming over us. The last thing Mom said to me was a collection of sounds I couldn't understand. The last word I remembered was "blinds," but the last sentence had been something she didn't really need to say anymore, really hadn't had to say for many years. She had said that she loved me.

"I know, Mom," I had said.

Her mouth still open, her head fell to the side.

"Did you hear me?" I said, and she had. She mouthed out the word yes, clicked the analgesia button on her epidural and sentences for her were one more thing in the past.

I remained next to her bed all day in that chair. Doctors brought me trays of stuff I picked at, and I was her present until it, too, was the past.

I so badly want to remember every bit of detail I can about Mom, Dairy, and Jean. It's an impulse, of course, brought about by my wanting Anne to know them, and, in the weeks after the accident, I'm disappointed to find that Dairy's house isn't haunted with her at all. But I have every intention of making it happen. In fact, I want all three of their apparitions to roam the space between the walls, crouch in the pantry, howl in the attic. I put up pictures of them all over the place in hopes of eliciting this and speak to them like roommates.

"Go ahead, Mom," I say. "I'm listening."

"I know," I say. "It's the consistency that matters."

"You look pretty," I say.

"I love you," I say a lot.

I'm no longer the same. I've gone over to some other side. In many ways, I succeed at being what I couldn't be for Anne the night of the accident. But it's an odd fit, and I'm still only part of who I was before I lost Jean and know that I will be for a long time. I am an echo. Later I'll be a voice. That'll have to be enough.

With the keys to Dairy's childhood place in the basket of Anne's stroller, I stand in Dairy's mother's kitchen. There are remnants of what it used to look like everywhere. The previous owners had updated various things, but I still feel like I'm on Dairy's set and make moves to return it to that state. I sink money I should have spent on other things into custom cabinets and vintage appliances. I play Dairy's videos to folks who look at me like some supremely sad creature at Home Depots and Farm and Fleets. I spend way too much time on Photoshop adjusting bland, 1980s coloring in Dairy's videos to look more real, or what I think real would look like now.

I have no idea what real looks like now.

A homecoming parade goes through downtown Morris. Football players on floats flex at the crowd. Hip-hop sizzles out blown speakers. Clicks of candy hitting the sidewalk, Anne and I are out in it. Kids wave and shouting cheerleaders approach in syncopation somewhere down the street. I reach under the canopy of the stroller expecting Anne to be upset, but she's content and sleeping. Overhead, birds spin between the buildings that line Morris' main drag.

One night when Jean and I were driving, we saw a blue heron cut above a tree line and fly, for just a moment, with a dozen or so seagulls. The birds were lit through their wings from the streetlights and spiraling wildly above this grocery store parking lot. The heron flew along with them, for just a rotation or two, and when the wind suddenly picked up, the heron shot off into the sky, a seagull trailing close behind.

Sometimes I drive Anne around in our car, her small noises bubbling up from the backseat, the dog huffing back there as well. I still drive too fast, but I do it on purpose, some ritual, to teach the importance of ritual, and I do it only when the corn is reaped, threshed, and I can see at least a mile into and over the fields.

On some mission, I'm out driving in this gray, overcast, but unseasonably warm October with Anne and the dog, roll down the windows, turn up the radio, have both hands on the wheel. The wind shoves us around, and I drive us all the way to Wallace, pull over in the spot where I'd lost Jean.

"You stay there," I say to the dog. He's curled up in the footwell behind my seat, some habit he's picked up since I've started taking him on our drives. He abides me, maybe knows I need him to, and settles into his spot without a fight.

I reach into the backseat, put some hat that someone sent me on Anne, take her out of her carrier and hold her in the wind that cuts across the county miles. She still won't make solid eye contact with me but her lids flutter. Her lashes wave like insect wings, and I shield her eyes with my hand, just stand in the country with her, Ottawa and Morris hidden somewhere within the trees off in the distance.

We're out there until the cool rain finally comes in. It starts with dots on Anne's shirt, and, sprouting up like wild dandelions, it splashes off her face. I know I'm supposed to keep her dry. I know I'm supposed to keep her warm, safe, but I leave the rain where it is anyway.

Because she smiles.

"Yeah, it's Mama," I say when she does.

Only after a while do I load her into the car, take us home.

As days pass, I find myself in this string of moments that have me trying to appear like the parent I would prefer to be until I'm emotionally able to actually be it. I begin to trust myself in ways I never have and Anne simply survives my vacillating interest in her, my fatigue and faltering will to get the whole thing right. I tell myself that feeling the way I do is natural because I have to, and, as she's forced to endure what could only be called my suspect abilities, I begin to gain some competency.

Because it's just another evening. I'm standing over Anne, changing her clothes. I feed her and, after she falls asleep in her carrier, I bring her with me to the kitchen, set her on the table. I take the timer out, put pots out on the stove, and turn on music that helps me think of Jean, Dairy, and Mom.

The music is too loud, and Anne wakes up, cries, rattles teeth. At first, I let it go. Her head buoys and sways in her carrier. So young, so animal, she's a strange thing to watch move. But, until she's her own strange thing, I suppose she's mine.

"It's okay," I say and slide a lid off one of the pots, fill it with water as Anne screeches and bangs around.

I relent, turn the music off, click the burner on, and, suddenly, Anne's head straightens up as if it's been anchored for the first time to the bottom of something, to something real.

She looks me right in the eyes.

In her, no matter how it makes me sound here, it's in that moment that I really do see everyone that's ever mattered to me.

But then she looks away, and I think she's so cruel.

I panic, click on another burner and she snaps right back to me as open flame waves.

I stomp up to her, stare into her eyes as long as I can in the hopes that she can see in me what I just saw flare from her. I have to believe that everything she needs to know about me transmits right there.

The soft wheeze of the burners behind me, this replicated house all around me, I lean over Anne. She blinks and her eyes wander off but immediately find me again, this time on their own. I back toward the stove and she watches me the whole way. I can feel her watching me, can actually feel her vibrate the space between us.

We look at each other and something about the exchange punctures me with how I'll one day loiter somewhere in Anne, too, that we all will, and I feel buoyant for a moment, but the kitchen's so still, so quiet, so nothing I hoped it would be. Of course there are no ghosts coming, no haunts. It's only my presence and Anne's. There's only where we came from, who we came from, those stories that manage to illuminate those people we loved, even hated, and, then, what we do with those stories, how we get them to illuminate us. It's Anne and I that are the apparitions that need to accept our state. It's Anne and I that haunt, and what we need to haunt is each other.

So, I start.

"OooOooOooOooOooOooOooOooOooO," I say.

She laughs.

I honestly didn't know babies laughed, but they apparently do. My baby did.

"OooOooOooOooOooOooOooOooOooO," I say again. I wave my arms around her carrier like the ghost I hope I can always be.

The dog barks at me, paws at my leg, and I settle back into myself. Steam erupts from the pot.

I don't do a thing to deserve it, but Anne laughs again, and I do too, right as I hit the timer, cook.

for Genevieve

ACKNOWLEDGEMENTS

Thank you, Chris Ott, Nick Stenzel, Matt Gallagher, Kiley Piercy, Rebecca Makkai, John Freeman, Paul Beatty, Lindsay Hunter, Heidi Julavits, Gary Shteyngart, Tenzin Dickie, Jeremy Ain, Arthur Seefahrt, Scott Dievendorf, Maryse Meijer, Steve Karas, Ryan Kanealy, Lincoln Michael, Michael Poore, Elizabeth McKenzie, Umberto Tosi, Adam Berlin, Jeffrey Heiman, Alan Ziegler, Martha McPhee, Tom McCarthy, Errol McDonald, Andrew Wilson, Caitlyn Tyler, Linda Swanson-Davies and Susan Burmeister-Brown, Jenni Ferrari-Adler, Brian Gray and Shane Singer – I wish you were here, Story Studio, the killer Chicago writing community at large, Purdue and Columbia universities and all my classmates there, my Novel in a Year cohort, Sam's Pizza, and all of those folks who spent time reading things I've written over the years and fought with me to get better. I know it was a fight.

I'd like to especially thank Janine Harrison who has always been in my corner. I'm deeply indebted to her.

I'd also like to show my deep appreciation for my parents, Paul and Linda Smith, who were my first editors, my brother Jeremy, and his wife Katy, and daughter Genevieve, as well as Liz, Paul, Clayton, and Dustin, the Nagler, Nemirow, and McCurdy families, and Gertie, the perfect dog. I love you all and am so grateful for you. Thank you for kindness, attention, and patience with me.

I, of course, really need to thank Jerry Brennan at Tortoise for choosing me and for connecting me with Lauren Gioe, who is simply the most kick-ass editor a writer could ever ask for. She's so generous with her mind and time. I couldn't appreciate either of you any more than I do. This has been a special publication process.

Lastly, thank you, Allison. You are everything to me. Before you, doing anything I thought valuable to do felt impossible. Since meeting you, nothing has. You've given me sure footing and the confidence and tangible support to go wherever I choose. You've patiently listened to every single rant I've ever had about this writing thing, rudderless and irrational or otherwise, and I simply couldn't do this, or much of anything else without you. I wouldn't want to. You've shown me the value of everything I care about. Thank you for being my wife. You're the most beautiful human on the planet. I love you.

About The Author

Ryan Elliott Smith is a veteran of the Army Reserves, a union carpenter with the Local 1027, and the editor of *The Broadsheet Journal*. He holds a BA from Purdue and an MFA from Columbia University. His story "Not Originally from New York or: The Misunderstandings" first appeared in *J Journal* and "Joining" was first published in the *Chicago Quarterly Review*. He was born in Ottawa, IL and lives in Chicago with Allison and Gert. He is currently at work on a novel about architecture preservationist Richard Nickel.

About Tortoise Books

Slow and steady wins in the end – even in publishing. Tortoise Books is dedicated to finding and promoting quality authors who haven't yet found a niche in the marketplace – writers producing memorable work that will stand the test of time.

Learn more at www.tortoisebooks.com, find us on Facebook, or follow us on Twitter: @TortoiseBooks.